BOOK SIX

THE
BOOK
OF THE
HEART

Carrie Asai

SIMON PULSE
New York   London   Toronto   Sydney

First Simon Pulse edition March 2004

Text copyright © 2004 by 17th Street Productions, an Alloy company

Interior illustrations copyright © 2003 by Renato Alarcao

SIMON PULSE
An imprint of Simon & Schuster Children's Publishing Division
1230 Avenue of the Americas, New York, NY 10020

 Produced by 17th Street Productions,
an Alloy company
151 West 26th Street
New York, NY 10001

Printed in the United States of America
10 9 8 7 6 5 4 3 2 1

Library of Congress Control Number 2003108405
ISBN: 0-689-86712-3
ISBN-13: 978-0-689-86712-5

To: *Nikkei Daily Business Desk* subscriber #45772
Cc:
Subject: Kogo Industries stock on the rise

SHARES OF KOGO INDUSTRIES STOCK SOAR

A positive note on the Kogo Industries front: Konishi Kogo's daughter, Heaven Kogo, who went missing four months ago after a brutal attack at her wedding in Los Angeles, is now reported alive and well and back in Japan. "Now that she is back, our attention is turned fully to business," says Mieko Kogo, Mr. Kogo's wife. When asked if Heaven was at home with her, she replied, "No, and I cannot say where Heaven is right now. She is being hounded by the press and we want to keep her as comfortable as possible." Sources say Heaven will definitely be in the Tokyo area soon, however, and this is definitely good news for the Kogo family.

It's good for the stock, too—shares of Kogo Industries, trading as one of the top 225 on the Nikkei Index, were at a low due to the uncertain fate of the company's chairman, Konishi Kogo. His brush with death and ensuing coma had investors speculating as to whether the business would remain as powerful as before. But now the stock is on an upswing. The company's acting chairman, Mieko Kogo, has taken the helm and cracked the whip. Sources say Kogo Industries VPs have been in nonstop meetings, working to streamline the business, cut costs, and boost production. Although she has not had any experience managing a global business in the past, Mieko Kogo says that she's had a lot of help. She has appointed her brother, Masato Seki, as vice chairman, replacing one of Konishi's veteran right-hand men, Kendo Matsui. "I'd like to keep the business in the family as much as possible," she says. "I know that Konishi would want matters run this way."

No doubt Heaven's homecoming has helped boost confidence in the company as well. Perhaps we will see her someday working for Kogo Industries?

Stay tuned for the next e-mail update at today's close of business. . . .

1

"This won't hurt a bit," said a voice in my ear.

I burrowed my head further and tensed for the pain. Strong hands pierced a muscle in my shoulder. They eased down to my middle back. I felt a hot twinge and squeezed my eyes closed.

"Ouch," I said. "That hurts."

No answer.

I was lying facedown on a massage table, a towel over the lower half of my body. The massage therapist's paper-thin Chinatown slippers were the only things I could see. The roar of an engine was the only thing I could hear.

I was on a plane, flying from L.A. to Japan. Flying home.

Across the cabin I could see my step-uncle Masato's shoes. I was lying too awkwardly to see his face. But his shoes—trendy dark blue loafers—kept tapping out an even rhythm, as if he had a song stuck in his head.

"Ow!" I said again. "I'm not supposed to feel this, I don't think."

"Have you been under a lot of tension lately?" the massage therapist asked. "Sitting at strange angles, perhaps in cramped quarters?"

"Um, you could say that," I answered. "On both counts." I'd just spent what felt like a lifetime in jail, spilling my guts to a cop and going on a botched sting to set up my ex-fiancé, Teddy Yukemura. If *that* wasn't tense, I don't know what tense is.

Masato's shoes still tapped out the same beat. I tried to put it to a song. It seemed like it was the rhythm of "Bootylicious," but I didn't really think Masato would be into Beyonce. Still, he seemed way hipper than my father, so there was no telling what kind of music he was into.

Then I heard another voice. "You must be so excited to be flying back to Japan, Heaven!" The owner of the voice wore thick-heeled platform sandals with a giant flower on top. Her toenails were painted a shimmery shade of green that she assured me was the "latest color in Tokyo." She had been introduced to me as Kaori, my uncle's personal assistant. And ever since I'd met her, which had been about two seconds before we boarded Masato's private plane, she hadn't shut up for a second. She made a huge deal out of the fact that now that I was flying back to Japan and would be under Masato's care, I had to have a complete makeover. Hair, facials, clothes, everything.

The therapist pressed her hands into another part of my back. She was doing shiatsu, which is a type of massage that concentrates on relieving blocked energy from the body. When her hands hit one of my pressure points, I sighed in unbelievable relief. It had been ages since I'd had shiatsu. My energy was probably blocked everywhere.

"I guess I'm excited," I said, my voice filled with uncertainty. I hadn't been back since Ohiko died. So many things had changed. Would I get to see my father? Mieko? What would happen to me? I honestly didn't know.

"Do not worry. You will be safe," Masato said from across the plane. "Try to relax."

"And besides, when we get back to Tokyo, we're going to go on a big shopping extravaganza!" Kaori said. "The Tokyo shops have great stuff right now. . . ."

"Okay," I said weakly. Shopping made me think of L.A. And L.A. made me think of Hiro. And that made me think of what Hiro had said to me, about who his family was. That they were connected to—entrenched in—the yakuza.

"You're tensing up," the massage therapist said.

"That's because you're pressing too hard," I muttered through my teeth.

"Your back is arching." She pressed on my upper back. "Just lie still." She'd found a knot in my shoulder and was pinching it in to release some of the tension. But the whole process hurt like hell.

Hiro was no better than Teddy Yukemura. And Hiro had *lied* to me. He'd lied to me for *months*. I'd . . . I'd kissed him! I'd told him I loved him! And he'd *lied*.

"Kutsugeru," said the therapist again. "You must relax. I'm going to put a lotion on your body now that will awaken your skin and chi. You can lie still and relax for thirty minutes, and then I'll start on your legs." She started to pull a screen around my table. The room grew dark.

"Now just let yourself fall. Let go completely," the massage therapist said.

I sighed and tried to clear my head. But then I heard Kaori speak from behind the screen.

"Heaven? Heaven?"

"Yes?" I answered.

"Where would you like to go first? Prantan Ginza or Takashimaya Times Square?"

"Either one, I guess," I said. "I think I'm supposed to be relaxing now."

"Oh, right. Of course."

I tried to imagine myself falling down, down, down. I'd been told everything would be safe now, but I still felt so keyed up. My mind flicked back to what Masato had said to me earlier when we were driving to the airport. He had led me from my jail cell in San Diego to his Rolls-Royce limo, explaining that we would be taking a private flight back to Japan. I'd climbed in the limo, bruised and quiet. He must have sensed my uncertainty because as soon as the limo rolled away from the curb, he put his hand lightly over mine.

"All your problems have ended," he said simply. "You're safe now."

I noticed right away, there in the limo, that he was the complete opposite of my father. Even the way he carried himself was different. My father would have sat in the back of the cab with perfect posture, hands folded neatly in his lap, no expression on his face. Masato, who had to be about the same age, sat slumped, sprawled against the seat, his feet constantly tapping. The tapping put me a little on edge.

"I don't quite understand why you're doing all of this for me," I said to him finally. "I mean, not that I'm not grateful, but . . ."

"It's my duty," Masato said. "You are family. Family must help one another. There are certain kinds of people in the world who cannot be trusted, who you will be free from now. You don't need to be grateful. This is duty, you see?"

I shuddered. *Kinds of people in the world who cannot be trusted.* Hiro.

"How soon will I get to see my father?" I'd asked. "Is he still in the hospital?"

Masato was quiet for a moment. "I respect your father, but he is not who you think," he finally said. "He has been putting you in danger. And there is something else—something you might not be ready to know, but I will tell you for your own good. There are people who are very closely tied to your father who don't want the best for you. Who would rather see you . . . hurt . . . or . . . out of the picture." He cleared his throat and shifted his weight closer to me. "These people are *very* close."

A shiver ran through me. "Oh," I said.

Wait, I told myself, snapping back to the present. *You're supposed to be relaxing. Letting go. Don't think about that stuff.* I closed my eyes again and tried to think basic thoughts: clouds, air, birds. Landing in Japan, Mount Fuji. I suddenly felt very light and airy. Maybe my chi was being aligned after all.

But then after a few more moments of bliss, I heard a voice. "Heaven?" It was Kaori.

"Yes?"

"You know, I think you'd look really great in Diesel. You don't have Diesel jeans, do you? Apparently Lucy Liu wore them all through *Charlie's Angels: Full Throttle*. There's a big Diesel store right in town. It's pretty new; maybe you haven't been there. Their jeans are *hot*! They have a whole new shipment in, I think. They have great shoes, too. We'll have to go as soon as we get back. . . ."

Relaxation came to a halt. I rolled my eyes in the semi-darkness.

We drove slowly through central Tokyo. I had been away only four months, but everything looked different. New stores had popped up in the place of old ones. And on every block Kaori pointed to some clothes shop, makeup emporium, record store, fitness club, spa, salon, nail shop, or jeweler that we had to go to as soon as possible. Masato spoke up front on his cell phone, murmuring in a voice so low that I couldn't make out anything he was saying.

I gasped when we drove up to Masato's compound. We pulled through the gates, past a lavish row of sakura, or cherry blossom, trees, a lustrous rock garden, and fountains. The house had several stories and was very modern looking. The front stone facade seemed to meld naturally into a waterfall. Giant goldfish swam in a clear, sparkling pond. The goldfish were as big as my forearm.

The limo came to a stop next to a line of three shiny, freshly waxed cars. Two of them were Mercedes. One was a Land Rover. The other was a sporty red Porsche Boxter, only my most favorite car in the world.

"Whoa," I said. "Nice."

"Isn't it great?" Kaori said as we stepped out. "I'll be living in the compound, too, attending to anything you need."

"Wow," I said again. They called it a *compound*. "How long have you had this place?" I asked Masato. "Weren't you in Costa Rica?"

Masato walked toward the house, ignoring my question. Then he turned back. "I'm sorry, but I won't be able to show you around. Kaori, however, knows the house very well and can show you everything." He smiled. "Make yourself comfortable."

I turned back to Kaori, who was pulling my bag from the trunk. There was nothing in it, really, except all of my essentials—money, wallet, fake ID, keys to Hiro's house and Cheryl's burned-down house, neither of which I'd been inside in ages, and a change of underwear.

Kaori inspected the bag. "This is all you brought?" she said.

"Yeah," I said. "I, um, travel light."

"Where's all your makeup and stuff? And clothes?" She cocked her head like a terrier, parting her lips a little.

"Well . . . ," I said. Did Kaori know nothing about what I'd gone through?

"If this is all you've got, we need to go shopping right

away," she said. "We'll have to make a list. But anyway, let me show you around."

All of a sudden I felt someone's eyes at my back. *Piercing* me. Trying to stay completely relaxed, I turned around slowly to look.

No one.

"What's the matter?" Kaori asked.

I looked right and left. And then I looked up. There, just under the eave of the roof, was the red eye of a video camera. I swept a gaze through the whole compound. Glittering video eyes extended as far as I could see.

I swallowed hard. We used to have video cameras in our house. But only at the front and back doors, for security. I remembered my father hadn't wanted to install them. He'd insisted that a bodyguard and dogs were good enough. But Mieko had insisted, saying cameras would make her feel much safer.

But these cameras didn't make me feel safe at all.

"Come on," Kaori said, ignoring the cameras. "Let's go to your suite first. We'll get you settled."

The red eyes followed me up a winding staircase into a separate wing of the house. The inside was as opulent as the outside: marble floors, expensive-looking furniture, ornate statues of Buddha in two different corners, strange art on the walls—huge paintings, canvases that were as big as the whole room. In one room there was a whole canvas of red. Some of the paint rose from the canvas in goopy globules. I shuddered. It reminded me of blood.

Upstairs on the walls were serious-looking black-and-white photographs of men and women. We got to one that looked familiar. I squinted. "It's Mieko," I whispered.

There she was in a frame, looking much younger, a sly smile on her face. Her hands were clasped in her lap. She didn't wear a wedding ring.

"Oh yeah, aren't these pictures crazy? Apparently they were taken by Akira Kurosawa," Kaori whispered. "You know, when he wasn't making movies."

"Do you know this woman?" I asked, pointing to Mieko.

"Sure," Kaori said flippantly. "I've seen her around."

A shiver went through me. *Mieko.*

"Do you know anything about her?" I asked.

Kaori glanced at me. After a moment she said, "Not really."

We passed another photograph of a man whose face was creased into a stern scowl. There was something about him that looked like Hiro. I squinted. Maybe it was his father? But why would a picture of Hiro's father be in Masato's house?

I couldn't ask Kaori; she was far down the hall. "Wait until you see your room!" she said.

I met her inside and gasped. Everything was bathed in white. An enormous feather bed, a white armoire, a big flat-screen TV in a cool gray. White curtains and carpet. On the white-tiled bathroom counter a neat line of white Kiehl's soaps and white-bottled Tommy Hilfiger and Michael Kors perfumes. Sephora and MAC makeup on a little shelf above the toilet. The tub a pearly white swimming pool.

"Wow," I said. "I had no idea Masato was . . . this rich."

"He's a very successful man," Kaori said, smoothing out the comforter on my bed.

"And . . . what is his business?" I said, not too loudly. I didn't know exactly what Masato did for a living, although I had heard he ran my father's business interests in Central America. But after seeing the entire mammoth house, the sports cars, the video cameras, the expensive electronic gadgets, I had a feeling Masato wasn't entirely legitimate. A nervous twinge rushed through me.

"Here's your meditation room." She pushed open a door to a little room practically made out of windows. I stepped in and looked around.

A white yoga mat was laid out perfectly on the floor. A fountain bubbled in the corner. A mirror went from floor to ceiling on one wall.

"I do yoga in the morning, and we could practice together in here if you want to do it, too," Kaori said, stretching her hands up to the ceiling.

We turned to the mirror. I looked at my reflection next to Kaori's. She seemed like a teenybopper in her bright green retro-looking baby tee and white Diesel jeans. Next to her, even though my chi had been rearranged, I still looked ragtag and exhausted. Hiro had given me a geisha cut a while back; it was starting to grow out and looked horrible. The short bangs were now getting long and fell into my eyes. My roots were black against the orangish blond. My eyes looked huge and cartoonish. I looked like a deranged Powerpuff Girl. Powerpuff Girl Gets Out of Jail.

"It's all so beautiful," I said. "I don't want to touch anything."

I slumped onto the bed and laid my head on the pillow. Kaori sat down next to me. "You know what else we should do?" she said. "Movies. I haven't seen a movie in like a million years. I was too busy flying over to the States with your uncle. The last good one I saw was *Full Throttle*. Have you seen it? Drew Barrymore looks adorable in it. There's this whole underwater submarine chase, and the angels are all wearing these crazy-looking scuba suits. . . . I just *love* them. . . ."

She chattered on. She seemed to have some weird obsession with the *Charlie's Angels* movies. I put my hands over my eyes. Why did Kaori so desperately want to be my friend? Didn't she have *work* to do?

"Kaori," I said after a while. "I'm sorry, but I'm really, really exhausted. I think I want to sleep."

Kaori stopped in midsentence. "Oh!" she said. "Of course. Goodness. You need to sleep. You must be totally jet-lagged. Okay, if you need anything, I'll be in the meditation room."

The meditation room had a window that looked right into my bedroom. Was she going to watch me from in there?

I sat on the bed for a minute, looking around the room. Not a hair was out of place. There wasn't a speck of dirt on the carpet. The pillows were white and flawless. It was the cleanest, purest, whitest room I'd ever been in. The whiteness made me think of Mieko. She would wear head-to-toe white around the house to please my father. White flowy dresses, white shirts, and even white shoes. I'd always thought she'd looked like a ghost in all that white. Her face was always so pale and serious; she never spoke. She floated around the house soundlessly. Sometimes I wouldn't even know if she was in the room or not.

As I gazed around the blinding white room, I could hardly catch my breath. I sat on a white bed, surrounded by white walls, with Mieko's eerie picture only yards away from me, too close for comfort. For a brief, shivery moment the room felt like a coffin.

It's strange to be here in my father's house. He built it with his materials, his hands. But there is more now. A bigger garden, an extra wing. New cars. When I called him saying that I was coming home, he seemed pleased.

My mother calls me into the chashitsu, the little room in the garden where we have our tea. She has always been relentless in getting the details perfect. Her life has changed since I was a little boy, but she has always had complete control over her tea ceremony. She is very proud of this.

She looks old; there are lines around her eyes. I wonder what the years I've been gone have done to her. For years I did not call them. I was told not to. I wonder what my mother knows. What she thought when I was away. Did she think I was dead?

"Purify your mouth and hands," she says in a soft voice, as if I had forgotten the steps of the ceremony. I wash my hands and my mouth. Then she leads me through the chumon into the tea room, which is set and lit with soft lanterns. Here we are in the spiritual world of tea. The physical world has dropped away. She slides the door closed; I latch it. We do this wordlessly.

She raises the fukusa and purifies the scoop and tea container. Her brow is relaxed, but she is in deep meditation. This is her only respite, I realize. This tea room. She must know a lot. She ladles the hot water into the tea bowl, folds the fukusa, rinses the whisk. She places three scoops of tea in my cup, then adds hot water. I nod.

Finally she speaks. "You look tired," she says. "Did you have a hard flight?"

"Not really," I say.

"What have you been doing all this time?" she asks.

"Working hard," I answer.

"Your body looks sound and strong," she says, taking a sip. "Your father says that there were some tasks you had to attend to while you were away?"

"Yes," I answer. "Yes, but that's done. I'm back now."

She nods, as if in approval. "Your father has been expecting you," she says. "He is happy that you've changed your mind."

I start to speak but stop. I am filled with so much misery for a moment that I can't even speak.

"He knew you would not stay in the United States forever," she says.

"Yes," I say.

"You look so tired," she says again. "What is it?"

What can I tell her? That I have thrown something away so precious—something that I will never get back again? That I must find Heaven, but if I find her, will she want me back? That I am having trouble choosing between what I love and what my family expects of me, even though I think it is wrong? I am not a bad person, but everything around me now is bad. Wherever I turn, there is evil. I don't know what to do. Any decision I make will be the wrong one to someone.

My mother and I don't talk about these kinds of things. And we especially wouldn't in the tea room. This is not the place. I sit back and close my eyes and hum softly, trying to ease myself into meditation. During the tea ceremony one must only talk about the significance of objects, the philosophy of the yin and the yang, the spirit of the tea.

"I just need rest," I say finally. And then in English: "And I need Heaven to understand."

She looks at me, her eyebrows raised. She doesn't understand English. We drink our tea in silence.

Hiko

2

Four days later Mieko came to see me.

Time at Masato's dragged by. It was like I was trapped in a day spa and I couldn't leave. Every morning Kaori greeted me with tea, fresh fruit, and scones. "Yoga?" she'd ask, putting the tray on my nightstand. She was so *into* yoga. She was one of those girls who made those huffing, breathing noises and really got into the poses. She could do the strength poses like the crow and the handstand. I knew yoga mostly from the training Hiro and I had done, and our yoga had been more vinyasa, or flowing. Kaori was into the hatha type, where you just sit in one pose for like an hour, suffering.

On the fourth morning after I arrived, Kaori and I were sitting in meditation. I wasn't really feeling it. I slumped out of the lotus position and let out a long groan.

"What's wrong?" Kaori asked.

"Nothing," I said.

Truthfully, everything felt wrong. It felt weird to be here.

Something felt just a little bit off-kilter, but I couldn't figure out what. I wanted to see my father. And worse, when I'd first gotten here, I'd been able to just block Hiro's confession about his family out of my head. But in the last day or so he'd started to creep back into my consciousness. I'd see a robe in the closet and think, *Wow, Hiro would think I looked hot in that.* Or I'd wake up and realize I'd just had a sexy dream about him. And then, two seconds after having a horny, longing moment, I'd remember, *Wait. I hate him.* His confession. His family. He was everything I'd thought he wasn't.

"You look like something's wrong," Kaori said.

"Nah, really, it's nothing," I said again. I didn't know if I wanted to confess any of this to Kaori. I didn't quite trust her.

She rolled out of her meditative position and leaned on one elbow. Then she arched up and stretched her left leg over her head. The girl was seriously double-jointed.

"So, today I thought we could maybe get a seaweed wrap. It's really good for cellulite." She looked over at me. "Not that *you* have any, of course, but . . . well, it's very detoxifying."

I wondered if she thought I needed detoxifying because of my behavior last night. While lying in bed, stewing over Hiro and watching an Ashton-Kutcher-a-thon, I'd asked Kaori if she could bring me a bottle of champagne. She'd brought us one, and I think she'd assumed that we would share it. But I'd drunk the whole thing myself. She'd sat on the chair next to my bed as I greedily poured it down my throat—from the bottle. I hadn't even bothered to get a glass. *The Godfather* had been on next, with Japanese sub-titles, which made it even easier to pretend that the characters on the screen were my family. Even though I really, really wanted to change the channel, I couldn't.

As I drained the bottle, Kaori had slipped quietly out of the room.

Needless to say, I didn't feel that great this morning.

"I don't know," I said. "I think I'll just go for a swim. Eat some fattening food. That dessert I had yesterday—what was it? A mousse? It was delicious."

Kaori looked at me skeptically but didn't say anything.

"So, anyway, what's the deal with you?" I asked her. "Where did you grow up?"

"Oh, here and there," Kaori said, not looking at me any-more. "So, listen, I was thinking maybe we could hit some of the shops today. . . . Maybe one of Masato's drivers can take us. . . ."

"Do you have a boyfriend or anything?"

Kaori perked her head up. "I think I hear my cell phone." Masato, though only in another wing of the house, con-tacted Kaori by cell phone whenever he needed her. She stood up. Her knees cracked. "I'll be right back," she said.

I sat in the room and stared at myself in the mirror. *Weird*, I thought. *Weird that she doesn't tell me* anything *about herself.* It was like she was a clone that Masato had created . . . like some freaky thing from *Star Wars: Attack of the Kaori Clones.*

The door slid open. Kaori stuck her head in. "You have a visitor downstairs," she said.

"I do?" I said, standing up. At first I thought, *It's my father. He's alive.* But then I remembered. Masato had told me Konishi was trouble. If it were up to Masato, I'd never see my father again.

Who could it be?

Kaori watched me nervously as I put on a black T-shirt and some plain but well-fitting black pants. She shredded a napkin from my breakfast to pieces. I slid on some slippers and padded downstairs.

As I approached the bottom of the steps, I realized who was waiting for me. How could I be so stupid? It was Mieko. It *had* to be. I just *knew* it. I sensed her presence. Hiro had told me time and again that a good samurai senses people before they can sense you. It was my haragai awareness coming through. The hairs on the back of my neck stood on end.

I saw someone sitting on a long divan in the living room. She wasn't facing me; I could see only the back of her shiny, black head. She wasn't wearing white, but it had to be her. I tried to stay relaxed. I didn't want her to know that I was down here quite yet.

She sat very tall and poised. I squinted and tried to get a look at the shirt she was wearing. It was black and had an interesting flower print and looked like it was made out of expensive silk. Then, in a flurry, she moved. I shot behind the wall. She picked up her purse—a bag I'd never seen—and rifled in it for a few moments. She lifted a tiny, slim cell phone out of the bag and looked at the screen. Then she threw it back in with an exasperated sigh and put the bag back down on the floor.

22

The bag looked expensive. Possibly a quilted Chanel. But wait, Mieko wasn't into Chanel, was she?

I crept up a little closer, using the shinobi-iri invisible walk Hiro had taught me long ago. I then caught sight of a high-heeled, pointy-toed stiletto shoe dangling off her foot.

I was floored. It looked like a Manolo.

What was Mieko doing wearing Manolos?

And then she turned. I froze.

"Heaven," she said, giving me a tiny smile.

I walked forward, frustrated that Mieko had caught me spying on her. "Hi," I said, trying to act completely natural.

"How are you?" she said. Her voice carried neither kindness nor love. It was a dead, meaningless tone. She picked up her bag again (it *was* a quilted Chanel!) and clutched it close to her chest, as if she thought I was going to steal it or something.

I was right next to her now. "Wow," I said. "You look fantastic."

She'd transformed since I'd last seen her. There were the shoes, the silk shirt, a pencil skirt, all in a sophisticated black. Her skin looked great and her legs were very thin and long— something I'd never noticed before. She looked like a model.

"Thank you," she said quickly, her face pinched and efficient.

I leaned forward to hug her, but all of a sudden she gave off this vibe that said, *Don't come close.* She still held the bag tight to her. I moved back and settled uncomfortably on the couch.

"It's good to see you," I said uncertainly. I felt a weirdness surround us, a rushing sense of panic. Something was wrong here.

She half smiled, then brought out her cell phone again. Her eyes flitted back and forth. I looked around. Where was Masato? Where was Kaori? As far as I could tell, neither of them was anywhere near this room.

Mieko crossed her legs. *God,* I thought. Who knew she was so thin? I wanted to tell her she looked much better in black than white but held back. She didn't look like she was in the mood for compliments.

"So," Mieko said. "How was your flight?"

How was my *flight*? "Um, fine," I said, and smiled. I felt like I was at a job interview or something. I clenched and relaxed my hands.

"And are you feeling well?"

Not that Mieko and I had been buddy-buddy when I was under her roof, but *come on.* "I'm fine," I said. "I had a little too much champagne last night, but you know. Sometimes it happens, I guess."

I laughed nervously. She didn't laugh back.

"So . . . how is he?" I said, taking a deep breath. "Is he still in a coma?"

"Well, yes," she said, flinching a little at the mention of Konishi. "Is my brother taking good care of you?"

What? "Um . . . wait . . . ," I said. "So Konishi's in a coma, then?"

She looked at me but didn't say anything.

"I don't understand," I said in a cracked voice. My throat grew dry. "Is there something I should know?"

Mieko leaned back. "I'm very sorry, but I came here in a rush." She looked at her cell for a long time. "I don't have any more time, so we'll have to talk about this later."

My jaw was on the ground. "But where are you *going*?" I asked. "Are you going home?" Konishi's house was a pretty long hike from Hiroo. She'd come here just to ask me how I was feeling? What the hell?

"I have something important to take care of," she said in her typical quiet Mieko voice.

"Are you going to see Konishi?" I asked. "Are you going to the hospital? Can I come?"

Mieko paused—it was almost like she was thinking about it. "No, now is not a good time to see him," she said shortly. "You must stay here until we get everything sorted out."

"Until we get *what* sorted out?" I demanded, raising my voice. "Why can't I see him? Where is he?"

She rushed out the door, slamming it shut. I ran up to the door and wrenched it open and peered down a hall I hadn't seen before. It was empty.

Kaori's voice rang out behind me. "Good visit?" she said in a chipper voice. I had the sense that she'd heard the whole thing. I was overcome by a sinking feeling. I didn't want to admit it to myself, but Kaori was nothing but a spy. She had no intention of ever becoming my friend.

"Take me to my uncle," I said, walking right up to her, getting in her face.

Kaori sputtered out a few syllables.

"I have some questions for him," I said. Anger bubbled up inside me.

"I can't do that," Kaori said finally. "I'm sorry. He's very busy right now."

"Where is he?" I said, stepping through the door and into the hall. Suddenly Kaori's hands were on my shoulders, pulling me back.

"I can't let you," she said, digging her fingernails into me.

"Get off!" I said, jabbing her with my elbow. For a little yoga-obsessed twerp, she was pretty strong.

I wrenched open the door. Masato appeared right in front of me. Kaori immediately got off my back and straightened up.

"Ah, hello, Heaven," he said, smiling calmly. "How are you today?"

I stopped in my tracks. Did he not know that Mieko had just been here? I peered around him into the room. It looked like an office, with a big oak desk and a fancy flat-screen computer. Mieko wasn't in there.

"I want to know that's going on," I said. "Right now."

"What's going on with what?" he asked, moving back into his office and checking out his reflection in the stately, oak wall mirror. He seemed bored, almost.

"Why can't I see my father? Where is he?"

Masato barely lost his cool expression except for one sliver of a second. In that second he shot Kaori a look of disdain. The look said, *You'll pay for this.*

"I want to go see him," I said. "And I want to know what hospital he's in. You must tell me."

Masato smiled again. "We can discuss this later," he said. "I have a very busy schedule."

"But I want to see him now!" I said.

"Heaven, calm down," he said evenly. "Your father is too sick for visitors at the moment. Any kind of excitement could be a serious shock to his system. Do you understand?"

I shot him a skeptical look. It sounded like bullshit to me.

"Just *relax*," he said. "Try not to think about things. Everything will be resolved soon."

"What does that mean? Resolved? What's wrong with him, exactly? I don't—"

"Heaven," he said, raising his hand and giving me a condescending smile as if I were a kindergartener playing with blocks. "You must stop this. Now if you'll excuse me, I need to get back to work." He shoved me gently out of the room and shut the door. I heard the clicking of multiple locks.

"Hey!" I said, banging my fists on the door. "You can't treat me like I'm six years old!"

"You shouldn't bother," Kaori said in a snooty voice behind me. "The room's soundproof."

I stopped pounding and glared at her. She glared back and then turned on her heel and stormed away. I stood in front of the door, staring at its thick oak exterior. I was being *lied* to. *Tricked. Something* was going on. Cool Masato no longer seemed as cool as I'd thought. And Mieko—what a freak show! I needed a plan. I needed to see my father and find out what was going on.

I banged on the door one more time for good measure,

almost near tears with frustration. Then I turned around, feeling an eerie sense that I was being spied on.

But it was just one of those damn video cameras blinking down from the ceiling. I glared up at it in rage. And then, in a rush of defiance, I gave it the finger. *Go to hell,* I mouthed. I didn't care who saw me.

My sister visits me in my office. I see her slight figure at the front door through the video cameras, and I watch her softly walk through the halls until she reaches my room. She hasn't changed since she was fifteen years old. Her skin is still perfect; her body is still tiny and totally fit.

She gives me a small smile. She does not wear head-to-toe white anymore. I told her a change would be best. Besides, all that white was too deathly, too eerie, too funereal. She's always had a strange fascination with death. But I arranged to have new clothes for her, a new edgy haircut, new shoes, new accessories. After all, she is now the company spokesperson. "A CEO must look stylish," I told her. "A CEO can't go around in white-nightgown-type outfits and expect to be taken seriously.

"She might want to escape," I tell her.

She lowers her eyes. "Yes," she says. "We have to get her before she escapes. We have to come up with a plan."

"But we have to make what's to come look like . . . a complete accident," I say, tapping my fingers on the table. "If our stockholders find out that we're behind this . . ." I trail off. My sister nods. She understands.

"She's looking for Konishi," I say. "This is why she is eager to leave."

She clears her throat. "Yes, but we could use that to our advantage." Her eyes meet mine. "There is a backup plan, too. I spoke to Kentaro Uyemoto today."

"Really," I say.

"Yes," she says. She keeps my gaze. "His son is back."

She pauses and picks up a necklace on my desk. "Isn't this a little valuable to have just sitting here?" she says in that scolding, older-sister tone. "Shouldn't you have it in a safe?"

"Costume jewelry," I tell her. Lying has become so easy to me now. "It's not worth anything."

She clucks her tongue. "All right. So where is she?"

"I just sent my assistant to get her. She'll be down. Wait for her in the sitting room."

"I'd rather not see her at all," Mieko says, fidgeting.

I nod. "Yes, but if you don't, she'll wonder what's going on. She'll escape before we can allow her to escape, you see?"

This Heaven is trouble. She asks too many questions. She suspects too much. Since the botched wedding she has become a woman. Not good for us.

My sister still looks worried. She bites her lip. "I'm not sure about this plan. Why ask your assistant to do this job? Are you sure we can trust her? And I am concerned about the Uyemoto boy, I must admit. He's feisty, from what I remember. He's like Ohiko."

"He's not quite like Ohiko," I say. "Ohiko had his own opinions. This one, even though he took off to L.A. for a while, has something inside him that makes him want to obey. He has made a wise decision, coming back."

"Duty to family is a hard moral code to break," she says. "At least for someone like him."

A knock sounds at the door. The assistant smiles at me. "She's waiting," she says.

"Thank you," I answer. She turns to leave.

"Kaori," I say, calling her back. I thread my fingers together. She turns back, questioning.

"I have a proposition for you," I say to her, and pull her inside.

Masato

3

The next morning my breakfast tray did not come as usual.

I had lain awake nearly all night, trying to come up with a way to get out of sight of the video cameras and Kaori for two seconds. I'd turned it over and over in my head. I could use my shinobi-iri method of invisibility. It had worked for me before. It could work again if I found the right shadows and if I caught people off guard.

I groggily staggered out of bed and looked out the window. Kaori was down at the pool, doing calm laps up and down, up and down. I'd never seen her in a bathing suit—it was a yellow string bikini to boot. She wasn't a bad swimmer. I scowled at her. The shadows around the pool were enticing. Many of them were deep and very camouflaging. I rubbed my hands together. They would be my way out.

I put on my T-shirt and a pair of low-waisted designer jeans that I found in the closet. They still had their price tag on: 24,000 yen, about $200. "Wow," I breathed. Funny:

before I'd gone to L.A., dropping $200 on a pair of jeans had been nothing. Now it was way more money than I had.

I grabbed my bag and my wallet and sauntered down to the pool. Kaori fluidly breaststroked the length of the pool, then turned and swam in the other direction. I stood under the awning; the deck was made out of fine teak, oiled and unblemished. I looked at it and thought, *Hiro said his father was in the lumber business.* I wondered how many Tokyo families were in lumber. I wondered where Hiro was. Just for a second.

When she popped her head out of the water midstroke and saw me, she stopped, standing in the shallow end.

"Hey," she said.

"Hmpf," I said back. I stood right at the edge. If I went now, it would take her a few seconds to scamper out of the pool and . . .

But in a flash she was at the wall and out of the water, next to me. She dripped all over my shoes.

"I'm sorry about yesterday," she said. She dropped her head. "And I'm sorry about this morning, not bringing you breakfast."

"It's cool," I said. *Run!* I told myself. But I couldn't. Something in Kaori's eyes really *did* seem sorry.

"It's just that, well, I'm just doing my job," she said.

"What do you mean?" I asked. "Is your job to keep me away from him?"

"Well, yeah," she said. "Basically."

"Do you know what's going on?" I asked. "Any of it? Do you know where my father is?"

Kaori walked over to pick up a towel. She had a good body and looked pretty strong. All those yoga headstands and handstands had made her arms exceptionally toned.

She dried off her hair and sat down. With the towel over her head, she spoke again. "I don't know much," she said.

"But you must know *something*. . . ."

She took a deep breath. "As much as I'm involved in your uncle's work, I don't get all the really inside info. So unfortunately I'm not sure what's going on with you and him at all." She sighed heavily. "And to tell you the truth, I'm kind of sick of my job. So I've pretty much stopped listening."

"Why don't you quit, then?"

"Your uncle took me out of a bad situation. I was in a lot of danger. So I owe him."

"What do you mean?" I asked.

She took the towel off her head. "My family didn't have much money. I . . . was in a compromising situation. He . . ." She gestured up to one of the top windows. "He saved me. Took me away. Gave me a job." Her lip started to tremble.

I sat down next to her. "What is he doing to you?"

She didn't say anything for a minute. "Nothing," she said. "It's nothing. I have to keep my voice down. I shouldn't have even brought it up." She pasted on that fake smile I'd seen all week.

She continued. "In any case, I'm sorry about yesterday. But you have to stay out of his way. He's doing what's best

35

for you." The whole time she said this, she kept that same smile plastered on her face. "Of course, if you want to leave, I'm not stopping you. It's not that I really like him much, even though he helped me out. He's not a particularly *nice* man."

"What's going on here?" I said nonchalantly. I didn't want Kaori to know how quickly the adrenaline was running through my body. "Is it something about my father? Are . . . are they going to kill me or something?"

She continued to smile. I couldn't tell what she was thinking.

"Kaori," I said. "Where is my father? Do you know?"

She didn't say anything.

"Come on," I said. "You must know something. You must *hear* something."

"It's ridiculous," she said. "If you go there, they'll know that I told you."

"Not if you come with me," I said. My head started spinning. "We could both escape him. You need a new job; I need to find my father. I need to at least see if he's okay. He might be able to help you."

Masato's words swam through my head: *Your father is not who you think. He has been putting you in danger. There are people who are very closely tied to your father who don't want the best for you.* Was that a bluff?

Kaori fidgeted with the edge of her towel. "I don't know," she said. She looked right and left. "Do you really think he could . . . help me? I mean, what kind of job could he help me get?"

"Do you know who my father is?" I said in a low voice. She nodded.

"He can do *anything*," I said. "He has so much money. What's your dream job?"

She didn't say anything.

"Come on," I said. "All you have to do is follow me and I can help you. But first you must tell me where my father is, or else his associates might pay you a very special visit. Who knows what will happen."

It was the first time I'd used my father's power to control someone. It was a complete bluff, and it didn't make me feel powerful. It made me feel cheap and nervous.

Kaori also looked nervous. She nodded. She peered up at the windows. The cameras were fixed squarely on us. *Please don't let the pool be bugged,* I thought.

"Tokyo Adventist," she finally said. "It's in Suginami-ku, on the Chuo line."

"Are you telling the truth?" I demanded.

She nodded slightly and then swallowed very hard. "Can I really come with you?"

"Yes," I whispered. "But let's go now. Just put on some clothes. Act natural."

Kaori walked as calmly as she could to her pile of clothes on the lawn chair. She took off her bikini, exposing her breasts to the cameras. Then she turned to me and slid the shirt over her head. She put her pants on.

"Come on," I whispered, moseying over to the cloaking shadows I'd observed from the window. I grabbed her hand as we reached them. "Mimic what I'm doing," I said, and

37

bent down. Within seconds we were both gone. And no one had seen us.

Or had they?

We would have to take three trains to get the hospital. Looking at the map in the Hiroo station, I started to get nostalgic for everywhere I *wasn't* going in Japan. First we would take the train one stop to Roppongi, where we would transfer to the Yamanote line, which snaked up the city and passed Yoyogi and its Meiji shrine, which honors the first emperor of modern Japan. My father had taken me there once when I was little. I remembered we'd wandered into Harajuku after that, and I'd just about died. It was the epitome of cool. Cool cafés, cool restaurants, cool little shops on narrow Takeshita Street.

Even though my father was Mr. Overprotective, there were times when we had a great time together. Usually it was when he took me shopping in Takeshita Street. Sometimes I could even get him to laugh, to let loose a little. It was always him and me shopping together, never Mieko. Ohiko would come along too sometimes and make fun of all the made-up, styled-out girls roaming the streets. He'd make cracks about the girls' high heels and weird Bo Peep outfits and strange logoed T-shirts. My father would have ended up laughing, and we'd always climb back onto the train happy and together. Almost a normal family.

Although Mieko never came along. Ever.

But there was no time to go to Harajuku. There was no time to check out the girls that Ohiko would have laughed at. My father wouldn't be there to say, "Ohiko, it's not nice to make fun," and then snicker despite himself. I slumped down on a bench near the platform, feeling very lonely, very disconnected. I also felt a little nervous. How sick *was* my father, exactly? Would I even *recognize* him?

I stood up and looked at the map again. The train would then pass Shinjuku, which I'd been *dreaming* about going back to for the noise, the lights, and the tall buildings. Finally we'd transfer at Nakano-Sakaue to the Chuo line, which, in one direction, leads out to Ryogoku's sumo stadium—another place my father enjoyed going. He always asked if I wanted to come with him, but I never did. Something about fat guys in little underwear made me feel a little nauseous. But we weren't going to Ryogoku. Adventist Hospital was at the Okikubo stop. I hoped it wouldn't take all day to get there.

On the walk to the station Kaori had told me the story of her past. "When Masato-san found me, I was working on the streets," she said.

"Like . . . ?" I raised my eyebrows. I thought of Kaori taking her clothes off in front of the cameras.

"Yes," she said. "I got in with the wrong crowd. Yakuza. It was bad. Very bad."

The question I couldn't ask hung on my lips. I looked at her expectantly, my heart speeding up.

"No," she said. "It was not through your father. Or anyone he knows. It was someone lower, dirtier. Someone with vague ties to the yakuza. Drugs and prostitution, that's all." She looked down. "I was a dancer, too, for a while. My big dream was to dance ballet." She laughed sarcastically. "Instead I danced around a pole."

"So how did Masato find you?"

"You realize that Masato is completely against yakuza," Kaori said, and then laughed bitterly. "He's like Spider-Man or something, avenging the people. He found me and dragged me out of all that. Offered me a job as his assistant. Told me that if I did a good job, he could maybe help me get into some ballet academies or even go to New York. Of course, that was three years ago."

"So he's kind of like a guardian angel?" I said.

"Oh, I don't know. I guess I should thank him for all this. But . . . he's not entirely respectful of me."

Now, on the platform, I saw the train whooshing toward us in the distance. I'd forgotten how *fast* the subway was here. The trains in L.A. putted along slower than a turtle.

"What does he have planned for me?" I asked after we got on.

Kaori didn't answer. "New York would be great, wouldn't it? I've always wanted to go to the top of the Empire State Building." She stared at the subway map, then grabbed my hand. "Heaven, before we go to the hospital, can we stop off in Roppongi at a travel agent's? It's the very next stop, look! I want to see how much a flight would be. If it's cheap and if I can get some help from your father, I'm going to book it." She smiled and hugged herself. "You have to start somewhere, right?"

"Wait, but we need to go to Tokyo Adventist . . . ," I said.

Kaori waved her hands. "It's, what? Noon? Visiting

hours aren't until three. Standard hospital practice. Have you ever been in a hospital before?"

I thought about it. I had been in the ER, I supposed, when the JAL flight had crashed. Not that I remembered it—I'd been a baby.

"Come on, come on," she whined. "The stop is next! We'll be really quick. Besides, Roppongi is so fun! I've been meaning to pick up a new manga as well. Do you read them?"

Of *course* Kaori would be into manga—she was like a manga character herself. I sighed. Kaori's life story was overwhelming. Was it really true?

"Well, I guess it wouldn't be too bad to stop in Roppongi," I said slowly. "I haven't been there in *so* long, it seems."

"Great," Kaori said, and smiled. She squeezed my hand. "Thank you."

"Aren't you worried about Masato finding out?" I said. "Following us? You seem awfully calm. . . ."

"Look, I told him that it was only a matter of time before I left for New York." She shrugged. "Life's too short. Besides, Masato's not a *killer*. I don't know what you're all twisted up about. I mean, he just didn't want to see your father in such bad shape, that's all. He was looking out for you, Heaven."

"I don't know about that," I said. Something Kaori was telling me didn't quite add up.

The train rolled into the Roppongi stop. Kaori pulled me off. "Two minutes," she said. "I promise. Then we'll take our nine million trains to the hospital."

Your father's in such bad shape. I tried to imagine my father, lying on a bed, shrunken and shriveled, breathing through a machine. I shuddered. Did I have the guts to go see him?

Kaori dragged me down the street. "Come on!" she said. The crowds were dense and crazed. Lights flashed. People spilled out of cafés. Kids played video games on the street. All around us was sound.

"Oh my God!" Kaori shrieked. "Morning Masume!"

We stood in front of a record store with photographs of the girl group Morning Masume splashed all over the front windows.

"I love them!" Kaori yelled, and grabbed my arm. "Let's go in!" She disappeared into a huge throng of people. They all looked like teenybopper club kids. Pink-haired girls sucked on baby pacifiers. A dreadlocked girl with bright blue eye shadow and a Naked Ape T-shirt jumped up and down. They all seemed to be in line for something.

I looked right and left. Where the hell had Kaori gone?

Wait. Maybe this was my chance to split. Maybe bringing Kaori along hadn't been such a great idea after all. I could get to Adventist by myself.

For one second I looked to my right and saw a boy who looked strikingly like Hiro. Same eyes, same hair, same height. I opened my mouth to say something, but then he turned and faced me. It was someone else.

God, I missed him.

I got on my tiptoes and looked for the door. Somehow I'd been swept into the middle of the room. Kaori had vanished.

I started clawing my way toward the exit, pushing past teenyboppers shrieking at nothing in particular. And then a hand rested on my shoulder.

I tensed and turned. But it was only a girl in pigtails. "Are you Heaven Kogo?" she said.

"Why?" I asked. Big mistake.

"Oh my God, it *is* you! Oh my God oh my God oh my God!" The girl clasped the arm of the girl next to her, who grabbed a guy standing beside her, who alerted about twelve other people. Someone started to grab at my hair, squawking, "Is her hair real? It's different than the picture!"

"It's Heaven Kogo!" someone else screamed.

The crowd parted. And past everyone's heads there I was, huge as a planet, plastered in blues and yellows and greens on the wall. My hair *was* different in the picture—it was before Hiro and I had cut and colored it.

Underneath my face it said, HEAVEN'S GONE.

And then, FUNKITOUT.

Shit.

"Heaven Kogo Heaven Kogo Heaven Kogo!"

"Help!" I cried. Random arms and hands were touching and pushing me.

"Get her up to the front of the store!"

"Does anyone have a camera?"

"Is it really her or is it an imposter?"

I looked desperately for the door. There it was.

"Suki, get over here, it's Heaven Kogo! Yes, from the song and the newspapers!"

Kaori was still nowhere to be seen. I made a mad dash,

kneeing and elbowing some people on the way. Hands dragged me back.

"No!" I screamed. I thrashed around, then planted quick blows to shoulders. People recoiled. I saw an opening ahead. "Let . . . me . . . out!"

The opening closed up with people. I ducked down, shinobi-iri style, staying close to the ground. I wove through the legs quickly, managing to get outside.

On the street I looked right and left. I had to move fast. I slunk next to the wall and found a shadow. As the crowd followed me, I slipped into an alleyway. It worked. Everyone rushed right by, thinking I was still ahead on the street.

I breathed heavily. For a minute my eyes couldn't adjust to the light. And then all five senses kicked in. I could feel that someone was there.

Something told me to run.

Then two people stepped into the light.

A huge, pockmarked guy. Looked yakuza. Holding a gun. And . . . standing next to him . . . *Kaori*.

"Ohhh . . . ," I said, stepping back.

"Heav-en!" Kaori called in a sickeningly sweet voice. I started to run.

"Come back here!" Kaori screamed, the sweet voice gone.

I tore through the streets. It had been a setup. What an idiot I was! I ran around a woman pushing a baby carriage and dashed across the street, nearly getting hit by a car. Someone on the next block almost plowed me down with his bicycle.

"Oioi!" he screamed. *Hey!*

I turned back. Kaori and the thug were hot on my tail. I heard shots ring out. Did he want to *kill* me? I looked ahead—oh God. The throng from the record store! Somehow I'd doubled back . . . and . . . there they were again!

"It's her!" said a girl in the lead.

I was cornered. I didn't know where to go. The Hard Rock Café loomed right in front of me. I had no choice but to go in.

I whirled inside to the sight of what seemed like thousands of American tourists sitting at glittery tables eating hamburgers and fries. A bunch of Japanese teenagers playing hooky stood at the bar, drinking Cokes. I looked right and left. The throng stood only feet away, outside, confused as to where I'd disappeared.

I gritted my teeth.

"May I help you?" the smiley, pixie-faced hostess asked me.

I shook my head and looked around.

I couldn't believe Kaori's expression back there. She was full-fledged yakuza. She might have been a dancer or a prostitute in a past life, but she'd had no intention of leaving Japan. It had all been a story just to get me off the train.

I wondered if there was a back way out of here. I could sneak out, grab the train, and then go up to Adventist on my own. . . .

Wait. Was my father even *in* that hospital?

"Oh God," I said, spreading my arms, trying to figure out

45

which way to go. But before I could decide, the yakuza thug burst through the revolving doors, waving a gun around.

Everyone in the restaurant except for me began to scream and climb under the tables. The hostess rushed off to the back room, maybe to summon the manager.

"Don't move," the thug said, staring at me. He ran up and grabbed me around my waist and swung me around so that my back was to his chest. The gun barrel nestled cozily to my temple.

The revolving door slid around again. Here came Kaori with her hands on her hips. She held a knife in her left hand.

"You can't escape," Kaori said.

"He's not even *in* Adventist, is he?" I spat.

She shook her head and laughed. "Oh, Heaven," she said. "You're so *naive*. You believe anything anyone tells you."

"*Bitch,*" I muttered.

She continued to laugh. "And we all *know*, Heaven, that your father is *completely* incapacitated. He can't *move*! He can't *breathe* on his own! She's told me time and again there's no *hope* for him! How is he going to help you or *give me money*? How is he going to . . . oh . . . sic his *thugs* on me?" She threw her head back in laughter. "You're *so* ridiculous."

I lunged at her, kicking out my legs. My foot missed her by about an inch. "*Who* told you there's no hope?" I shrieked. Kaori had said *she*.

"Hey, settle down," snarled the thug with the gun, pulling me closer.

46

"No!" I screamed. "I won't shut up!"

The crowd had reached us by now and had all piled into the restaurant. Once they saw the gun, they stood back. They formed a loose circle around Masato's thug and Kaori and me. One brave girl shouted, "What are you doing to her?"

"None of your damn business!" Kaori screamed, showing the knife to the crowd. "Leave, now!"

"Help me!" I screamed. "Someone! Call the police! Keisatsu! Where's the manager?"

"Keisatsu," Kaori said, laughing again. "The *police*. That's a good one."

The thug cocked the trigger and drove the gun further into my temple. I bit my lip. Then I saw Kaori look over at us and shake her head vigorously. What did that mean? She mouthed something. It looked like, *It's too crowded. Let's take her back.*

"What's happening?" I said, my voice wavering.

I looked around frantically. I saw no Hard Rock staff members. Elvis buzzed loudly through the speakers, singing, *I ain't nothin' but a hound dog,* as if this all wasn't taking place. The patrons still crowded under their tables.

"Someone do something!" I screamed. "Please! Help!"

"All right, that's enough," the thug barked. His arms became tighter around me, and all at once a dull thud hit my head. The distinct scent of curly fries, slathered in ketchup, became very strong. Then the pain set in. And then I fell into a black, dreadful unconsciousness.

4

I was walking through the garden at my father's house. There was a stone path surrounded by artfully crafted bonsai trees. Ahead I saw my old house. *I wonder if Mieko is inside,* I thought.

I began to walk toward the house. The leaves were falling rapidly off the trees. I looked at the window and saw Mieko's silhouette—and someone else's, too. I couldn't make out who the other person was.

A figure stepped into my path. Teddy. "Hello," he said. He wore his typical Teddy getup: oversized Ecko Unlimited shirt, low-rider dark denim pants, Adidas shell tops. "How's my girl likin' bein' back in the crib?"

"What are you doing here?" I said in a hushed voice. "You're supposed to be in hiding or something!"

"*Am* I?" he answered. "Who says so?"

"Remember? The police setup?"

"So you found out about your boy Hiro, huh?" He

stroked his chin. I noticed he had the beginnings of a goatee. "Pretty rough, I'd say. Although I could've told you about it all along."

"So why *didn't* you?" I demanded, hands on hips. "How deeply is he involved in all this? Has it been a setup—me and Hiro—all along?"

"Nahhh," Teddy said. "It's just a coincidence." He shrugged. "Actually, I have no idea." He looked me up and down. "Damn, you lookin' *fine,* girl! Did I tell you last time I really like that thing you did with your hair?"

Something looked different about Teddy. I couldn't quite put my finger on it. And then I realized. He had a third eye, growing out of the center of his forehead. I heard Kaori's yoga-chanting voice from somewhere, saying, *Harness your third eye. Reach out to your third eye and you can channel peace.* I reached out to touch Teddy's third eye, but he instantly turned to molten lava, burning me on contact.

I screamed and then sat up in bed. I was covered in sweat.

Where was I?

I looked around. It was my room at Masato's. I quickly flashed back to what I could remember: being surrounded by Masato's thugs, Kaori, pain, then nothing.

I felt woozy and my mouth was numb. They must've drugged me so I'd sleep for a while. I looked at my watch: 7:45. Even though it was dark, I wasn't sure if it was A.M. or P.M.

Groggily, I lumbered to the bathroom. God, that dream had been weird. It had been like Teddy was, I don't know, more *realistic* than people were in most dreams. I mean, aside from the third eye bit. But I'd felt like he was right there next to me, actually talking to me. I'd thought I felt his hand take mine; I'd thought I felt the leaves under my feet.

I stared at myself in the mirror. Lovely. Another black eye. I groaned. How *stupid* had I been to include Kaori in my plans? I'd thought that she seriously wanted out—who in their right mind would want to be an errand girl for creepy Masato? But God, I'd known better, and I'd gone along with it anyway. All this time something had been telling me that Kaori was trouble, but I'd let the emotion of possibly seeing my father get in the way. . . .

All the progress I'd made with assessing and controlling situations—I'd managed to overpower Shigeto and maybe help him with his drug problem back in L.A., all because of harnessing my haragei. Now I felt like I was back to square one. I could imagine Hiro pursing his lips and shaking his head.

Hiro's gorgeous lips. I wanted to start crying again.

A knock sounded at my door. I raised my head. Great. Was this the firing squad? What were they going to do to me? *Haragei,* I told myself. *Get control. Activate every nerve.* I had to get out of here, and I had to formulate a solid plan that would get me out fast.

Before I could open the door, Kaori whisked through. "Hello!" she cried. "How are we this morning?"

I didn't answer. "Bitch," I muttered under my breath.

She carried a tray of tea and udon and dumplings. "I brought you some stuff—you were really knocked out! Must've been tired. Get a good rest?"

I looked suspiciously at the tray. "Is this stuff poisoned?"

Kaori looked genuinely shocked. "Of course not! How could you say such a thing?"

My God, she was weird. "Come off it, Kaori," I said. "Why should I even speak to you? And stop patronizing me with that pathetic act of yours."

Kaori sat down on the bed. "Look, I'm just doing my job. You understand now that if you don't cooperate, you'll force us to make your life miserable. And we don't want that. We want you to be *comfortable* while you're here. Now, how about a massage today? I've scheduled us for a sea salt facial as well. It's at three. Perhaps you want some time alone? I'll see you then."

"Why did you even string me along and get me on the train?" I asked, although I had a pretty good idea why.

Kaori turned, not answering. To torture me, that was why. I thought of that thug with the gun. Perhaps to get me in public and then . . . to kill me.

Oh my God.

I sat on my bed and gnashed my teeth for a while, realizing I hadn't grilled Kaori about her little slip yesterday—what had she meant when she said, *She's told me there's no hope for him*? I was so forgetful. What, were they putting something in the water around here? I gulped.

I stood in the middle of the room and did some tai chi warm-ups to activate my nerves and heighten all my senses.

I had to get out of here.

I followed through with kicks and punches, pretending they were Mieko's face. Was Mieko the *she* Kaori had meant? Mieko definitely was up to something. Why was I not allowed to see my father? What was the big cover-up? Why had Masato told me back in the States, "Your father is a strong man—he will recover," and now he was totally anti the whole thing? My head spun.

I moved on to some roundhouse kicks, nearly knocking over a lamp. *We just want you to be comfortable while you're here.* What if . . . I don't know . . . what if they were slowly killing my father, or at least keeping him permanently in his coma, right under my nose, in a different Tokyo district? I stood completely still. I felt every nerve come alive. *Something is wrong,* my body said. *Something is terribly wrong.* I felt my haragei working.

"Oh, no," I wailed, and shoved the door open, fluttering past Kaori, who was lying on the couch in the room right outside mine, reading a book.

"Where are *you* going?" she asked.

I didn't answer her but fled down the stairs. I could hear Kaori following me. I reached the bottom and came upon the room where I'd met up with Mieko. I looked right and left. There were two different corridors—which way to go? I scrambled down one, sensing that Kaori was right behind me. I ran so quickly, I nearly tripped over my shoes. I wrenched open a door and behind it was Masato, working on a big computer.

"Heaven!" he said. "What a nice surprise. But I was not made aware that you would be visiting me."

"I need to talk to you right now," I said.

He smiled in a way that someone might smile if they were being given a thorough back massage. Calm, relaxed, Zen. "Ah, yes. Well, I'm a little busy."

"What is going on around here?" I asked. "What are you doing to my father? Why was some guy with a gun following me yesterday?"

"All right," Masato said. "Come in, we'll have a little breakfast. I was just in the middle of mine."

I followed him into his room. A large fruit salad on a tray was perched on the end of his desk. He had the weird big computer and a whole bunch of silver, high-tech-looking gadgets. About twenty television screens were on the left wall. They were all blank. Could those be the screens to the video cameras? I looked at them anxiously, waiting for a picture to pop up. None did.

"So, you are wondering about your father," he said, weaving his hands together. "I realize this, Heaven. But you have to trust me. Your father is not dead, your father is not in danger. But *you* will be in danger if you try to see him. Did Mieko not explain this to you the other day?"

"No," I said, dumbfounded. "She barely said anything to me at all!" As I said this, a thought glimmered through my head: He *had* known that Mieko was here. Whether he knew it or not, he'd just slipped, slightly. Before, he hadn't let on that he knew she'd visited. *They're up to something together—I know it now.*

"And that man was not intending to shoot at you," he said, stabbing a piece of kiwi with a chopstick. "He was protecting

54

you from the crowd. They were quite hostile, I hear?" He smiled slightly.

"Oh, *that's* a good one," I said. "Don't insult me."

He stayed silent for a moment, contemplatively chewing on a piece of mango. "Have you been able to relax at all? Members of our spa staff are among the top practitioners in Japan."

I didn't answer him. On his desk was this humungous diamond necklace. Seriously, the thing was as big as the Hope diamond. Why did he have it just *lying* there, unprotected? Didn't he worry about it getting stolen? Was it fake? It sure didn't *look* fake.

Masato continued. "You know, I am thinking of taking a business trip to Thailand quite soon," he said. "Perhaps you would like to come. It would be a wonderful change of scenery for you."

I wrenched my eyes away from the necklace. "I just want to see my father," I said.

He shook his head. "Soon, Heaven. I assure you, doing so now would put you in danger."

"Danger how?" I demanded to know. "In L.A. you said you would have answers soon. So what's going on? Why can't I know anything?"

"Kaori could come along too," he said. "You two could girl talk together. How fun would that be?" He smiled and took a large bite of a pomegranate.

My mouth hung half open. This was like talking to a wall. I felt light-headed all of a sudden. Light-headed and trapped. This wasn't helping me at all. I had to get out of here, fast.

My stomach growled; my worries about Kaori poisoning me had caused me to skip breakfast. As *if* I'd want to girl talk with her. I grabbed for a piece of pineapple. I took a gigantic chunk and shoved it into my mouth. Masato smiled icily.

"Lovely," he said. "Well, enjoy. And let me know what your thoughts are on Thailand. That is, if you'd like Kaori to come or not. Perhaps you'd like another person. Did you get along well with Greta, the masseuse?"

I stood in his doorway. And then, all of a sudden, I felt that weird nerve thing again. My whole body felt like it was connected to a megawatt tower. My eyes were on fire. Masato sat there, calmly eating his breakfast, looking at his computer. *He's doing something terribly wrong,* the sense told me.

I saw my father lying on a bed. I saw Masato and Mieko standing around him, adding something to his IV drip. I didn't see a doctor. My father's eyes were shut; his limbs had grown weak. Masato and Mieko smiled at each other darkly.

And before I could control myself, I lunged back into his office with a flying kick to his head.

"Hey!" he shouted. I grabbed him around his neck and held him, but then, in a move I was unfamiliar with, he spun me around. Suddenly I was up in the air and he held me by the shoulders. Masato used one hand to press a button under his desk.

"Now you've gone too far," he said.

I turned my shoulder and got out of his clutches, landing awkwardly on my ankle. I started battering him again, but suddenly his door flew open.

Two big guys with guns pointed at me stood, waiting.

I froze, breathing heavily.

Masato crossed his arms over his chest. "Will you ever learn?" he asked. He nodded to the guards. "Take her to her room," he said. He shot me a sinister look. "No relaxing for you today!" Then he sat back down and ate another bite of fruit.

The guards seized me. I kicked and flailed, but they easily held on. "You're killing him, aren't you?" I screamed. "You and Mieko? You're killing him! And I'm next!"

They put a blindfold over my face. And tape over my mouth. I screamed out muffled cries as they dragged me from the room.

They hauled me up the stairs and turned in a bunch of directions. Finally I felt them releasing my arms. I fell in a heap onto what felt like a pile of sweaters. I heard a door slam behind me. Quickly I tore off the blindfold and tape.

Pitch blackness.

Where was I?

I looked around. The light was dim. My head ached. I tried to stand, but my head hit something. It felt like shirts. I reached up and felt a bar. Then I felt hangers. And more shirts. And jeans.

I was in my closet.

I felt like crap. *Another stellar move,* I thought. *Way to go. That's the way to get out of here sneakily—to beat up Masato.* I tried the closet door. It was locked.

Shit.

They'd locked me in the *closet*?

I jiggled the door again. Apparently they'd managed to lock it from the outside. Great. I took a deep breath. My stomach growled; my head throbbed. I felt disoriented and slow. I knew it was wrong of me to have gone after Masato, but I'd never had an *instinct* like that before. It was like . . . it was like a message from God. I knew that Hiro would say, "No, you are just hyperaware—you were reading Masato's mind. You saw inside his head. You saw what was going on."

I hoped that *wasn't* what was going on. My fists balled up in rage. I curled and uncurled my toes, frustrated.

Footsteps. Was it Kaori? I wondered if she'd get me out. In a way, I didn't want her to be the one to save me. "Thailand," I grumbled under my breath. Masato really was insane.

But instead of Kaori, I heard two maids walk into the room. I pressed my nose to the closet door and peered out one of three narrow slats near the top. They held piles of sheets in their arms. At my bed they dropped them on the mattress and rushed to clean up the pieces of china that must have broken when the guards threw me in the closet. "Messy girl," one of them murmured.

I didn't know whether to make any noise. They moved around my bed quickly, putting on new sheets, a luxury I hadn't been able to afford in the States. At Hiro's, I'd slept on the couch. At Cheryl's, my sheets had been washed when my clothes were, which wasn't too often.

"The little princess has crumbs in her bed," the other maid said, shaking out the sheets.

"She's probably never learned to clean up after herself," the first one said.

Okay, half of me was dying to just burst out right now, fists flying, and say, *Why don't you repeat that, bitches?* Then I'd kick them both in the jaw so that they'd flip over backward. The looks on their faces would be priceless.

They murmured for a while—they were doing the whole shebang, vacuuming, dusting, even cleaning the slats in my blinds. I prayed they wouldn't come into the closet. And then they started speaking in lower voices. I strained my ears to hear.

"So guess what Tacho told me," said one of the maids, a woman with her hair in a bun.

"What?" the other, portlier woman asked.

"He said that he had to make a run over to the Yukemura compound."

My ears pricked up at *Yukemura*. Tacho, if I remembered correctly, was one of Masato's drivers. *Yukemura!*

The woman in the bun continued. "When he was over there, you know who he saw? Hiro and Kentaro Uyemoto."

"No!"

"It's true!"

I felt that one little chunk of pineapple rise in my throat. Did she say . . . ?

"It's big news, you know, because the son hasn't been in Japan since he was asked to leave! Four years ago!"

"Is he back for good?"

"Apparently. Rumor has it he is joining up with his father."

What?

The portly maid giggled. "I always thought he was so handsome."

"I saw him once," said the girl with the bun. "He came with his father four years ago over to the compound! He was much younger then, but yes, still handsome!"

I did everything in my power not to make any noise. These biddies were joking and gossiping about Hiro and his father like they were characters on the *Sopranos*! I doubled over, nauseous. Hiro was back with his father. I wasn't ready to hear this. I covered my mouth with my hand, afraid my stomach was ready to empty itself.

And Masato's driver had been there. Meaning Masato must've been there, too. At the Yukemuras, like one big happy family.

My head spun even faster than it had when I was in Masato's office. Everyone was conspiring against me. Kaori. Mieko. Masato. The Yukemuras.

And now it seemed like Hiro was in on it, too.

I had to get out of this closet right now. I didn't even care if the maids were still in the room. I pulled on the door. Something was keeping it locked. Okay. I breathed in and mustered all of my strength into my arms and legs. I backed up into the denims and the silks and the cottons and took a few steps forward. I raised my arms and shot out my foot. Luckily, my foot had become pretty calloused from all the practice. But the door was heavy and kicking it would be painful.

"Ahghh!" I screamed, putting all of my strength into the

kick. Amazingly, it worked. Wood splintered and I heard something recoil and snap on the outside. Pieces of the closet door went everywhere. And suddenly I could see my bed again.

I looked around. The maids were gone. There was no sound anywhere. No one had heard me.

I sat down on the bed and put my head in my hands. Anger had gotten me out of that closet. Now tears of anger ran down my cheeks. I was a prisoner in this room, I was a prisoner in this house, and my time with Hiro had been a setup. Nothing, and I mean nothing, was real anymore.

Kaori found me lying like an *X* facedown on my bed. "What happened to the closet?" she said, looking at the mess of splintered wood. I didn't answer.

"It's like the Incredible Hulk was in here or something!" she went on.

I'd had just about enough of this. I was going to make a break for it. Tonight. I felt that I finally had my wits about me. I wasn't going to tell anyone. There was just one thing I needed to do before I left.

That diamond necklace. The one sitting on Masato's desk. I had to get in there and take it. I could pawn it when I was out.

"Why haven't you eaten anything?" Kaori asked, looking at my breakfast tray.

"I don't feel well," I said, even though that wasn't exactly true. I was famished. I was way past the point of being blood-sugar crazed. I was ready to eat the *sheets*. I didn't want to eat what they were bringing me. If they could slowly poison my father, why wouldn't they want to slowly poison me, too?

"I brought some episodes of *E! True Hollywood Story,*" Kaori said, holding up the DVDs. "I think I have Drew Barrymore, Cameron Diaz, and—"

"Let me guess," I muttered. "Lucy Liu?"

"How did you know?" Kaori said, grinning. "Want to watch?"

I shrugged. "Whatever," I said. We didn't speak through the entire Cameron Diaz episode. The only other noise that echoed in the room was the growling of my stomach.

One episode in, I faked sleep. I snored louder than a buzz saw, and every time I let out a grunt, Kaori jumped about a mile in the air. Finally I felt her weight lift off my bed. I opened my eye a crack. She left the room and shut the door tight. I heard a sharp *click* of a key—she'd locked it from the outside.

Shit.

As soon as she was gone, I sat up. Eleven-thirty. I ran to the window. That idiot. She'd locked me in here, but the window was wide open. I paced back and forth, waiting for a little time to pass. I didn't want Kaori to check on me and find me gone.

After a few hours I slung my bag over my shoulder and looked back at my room. *Hasta la vista.* I wiggled out the window and hung by my hands from the bottom frame. I looked down—a video camera eye slowly rolled over to me. I flattened my body up against the house in the shadows. *I am invisible,* I repeated to myself.

I kicked out to a large tree next to the window and slowly shimmied down. I had a problem with heights, so the view made me a little nauseous. I needed Spider-Man webs so I could stick to surfaces and not fall.

On the grass I took a deep breath and ran into the house through the back patio door. It was still open. The downstairs lights were off, but the hallway was lit by blue nightlights. I crept close to the wall until I found the door to Masato's office. Locked. I rooted around in my bag for a lock pick—Hiro had taught me how to pick locks once, explaining that in some situations it was necessary. I inserted the metal rod into the doorknob, felt the lock, lifted it up, and twisted my wrist. I tried the door again, my breathing shallow. It worked. I was in.

Masato's computer was off, but all the video cameras were on. I could see him sitting on his bed; I could see Kaori sleeping on the couch in the room outside mine. I ducked down as soon as I saw them, staying close to the floor. If there was a camera in Masato's room, there definitely could be a camera in here.

I grabbed the necklace as quietly as I could and shoved it into my pocket. I slunk down to the carpet again and wormed my way to the door. Something about even this *room* made me feel uneasy. It was as if Masato's chi filled it up and made it evil.

Out on the lawn again, I had to go a direction that wouldn't set off Masato's alarms. I looked right and left and then got the feeling I was being watched. And *not* by a video camera.

I swung around. There was the figure in the bushes. A tall figure—a thug? Shit. I bit my lip. I braced my body for contact.

But when I tried to assess who it was, *thug* didn't come to mind. Something else did. Something warm and nervous instead. A feeling of electricity washed over me.

The figure stepped partially out of the shadows.

"Get back," I whispered, fingering the heavy jewels in my pocket. "I'm armed."

But then he stepped completely into the light. First I saw his hair, then his shoulders and torso, and then, completely in the light, his face. My mouth dropped open.

It was Hiro.

My father comes to see me two days after the tea cere-
mony with my mother. This is our second important talk.
During the first one we went through all the major players:
the Yukemuras, the Kogos. Various other families. I asked
him casually about what I'd heard about Heaven. About her
past. I was looking for confirmation of the truth.

My father is no longer a laborer but a businessman. He
has not been a laborer for a long time, of course, since back
before he built up his company from nothing. But he still has
the strong, rough hands of a man who knows what real work
feels like. He always used to say this to me. Know the weight
of real work, son. It will make you grateful and humble.

Now he wears business suits of the most expensive cal-
iber. He carries a mobile phone. He is gray at the temples
and wears little glasses. I try to imagine him in a lumber-
man's uniform, and I can't.

"I will forgive you," he starts, "for your past mistakes.
And I see that your coming home has meant you finally
want to join the business."

I nod slightly. I feel weak, but I need money. L.A. is not
providing me with anything anymore. I have given up, in a
way. I feel empty without Heaven. These last two days I've
paced moodily around my room, trying to figure out what to
do. How could I get her back? How could I get in good stead
with my family? There were no answers. I was floundering
alone in L.A. Losing my family was one thing, but losing
Heaven weakened me to the bone. I have no resolve now.

But in some ways the fact that she rejected me makes
me angry. Why does she have the right? How dare she get

mad at me for admitting that I come from the same back-ground that she does? How dare she get mad when I tell her the truth—that I am tempted, sometimes, to go back to that life, at least for the security? Why didn't she let me explain what kind of life I was talking about? Instead she just bull-dozed ahead, assuming the worst, and hung up on me.

Why does she think that I'm as pure as snow? That I'm not like any other man? That I'm free of weakness?

My father clears his throat. "Two things. One, the initia-tion is set for tomorrow night. I assume that is fine with you."

The initiation. *I gulp.*

"And two, Masato has a favor to ask of you. Has he dis-cussed it with you?"

I nod.

"Do you understand why it must be you who does this?"
I nod again, this time even more slightly than before.
"What if I say no?" I ask softly.

He chuckles. "Son, what will you do? Say no? And then what? Where will you go? You had no money to get back here—why would you have any money to go anywhere else?" He smiles smugly.

"And besides," he says. "It is the aim of samurai chil-dren to fulfill their filial duties. Honor your parents. An ancient sage once said, 'Look for loyal ministers in homes with filial sons.'"

"This hardly concerns the samurai way," I reply. "This is about something else."

He crosses his arms over his chest. "If you do not join

with me and do what Masato says, your life is out of my hands."

I say nothing.

"It's settled, then," he says, standing. Before he leaves, he turns and smiles. "Ah, I forgot to tell you. Dinner is in an hour."

Like a good son, I thank him.

Hiro

5

"Don't come any closer," I said. "This place has about a million guards. You'll be dead in seconds."

"And what are *you* doing out on the lawn, then?" Hiro asked. "I'm not here to hurt you; I'm here to help."

"Yeah, sure!" I said. "What do you take me for?"

"Keep your voice down," he said. "You're talking crazy. I came to get you. You're not safe here."

"Stay away from me," I said. "I mean it. Who ordered you to kill me? Was it Mieko? Or maybe Yoji Yukemura? I heard about your *meeting* today."

"What?" Hiro said. Then he sighed. "Heaven . . ." He reached out for my hand, but I pulled it away. "There are a lot of rumors swirling around right now, but anything you've heard inside Masato's compound is definitely double-talk. Who told you I was going to kill you? Who told you I was siding with the Yukemuras, of all people?"

"*Someone,*" I said, feeling a little foolish that it had

just been two gossipy maids. "Someone who *knows*."

"Don't you realize that anything people say in this place is because *Masato* wants them to say it? I'm betting you heard this from a servant or something; am I right?"

"No," I said, a little too quickly.

"Don't you think whoever you heard this from—don't you think Masato told them this for the exact purpose that it *would* get back to you so you wouldn't trust me?"

Hmmm. He did have a point. Believing anything that was said in Masato's compound was probably idiotic.

"Come on," Hiro said, extending his hand again. "We have to get out of here before someone sees us. You're in danger. Masato and Mieko are doing terrible things. You'll be killed if you're here for much longer."

Something about his voice chilled me to the bone. I looked at Hiro, standing there. I hadn't seen him since I'd gone to jail. His hair was still cut the way we had done it when we'd gone "undercover." It was much trendier than usual, grown out and spiky, kinda Brit pop, kinda club kid. He looked gorgeous. He also looked sincere. He didn't look like he was here to kill me. Still, there was something wrong about him. There was something behind his eyes that I couldn't quite understand.

"Come on," Hiro said. He started walking to the pool. "I love you, Heaven. I came to Japan for you, not for my father."

I wavered. I didn't know what to believe. But I knew for myself that Masato was bad news. A psychopath. If I stayed here, I *would* die.

"All right," I said. "But leaving with you means nothing. I was going to leave anyway."

We crossed the pool silently. I watched Hiro, feeling a little out of it. Suddenly there was a violent shriek from what sounded like my window. "She's gone!" It was Kaori's voice.

"Kaori," I whispered.

"Who?" Hiro asked.

"Just run!" I said. "This way!"

Sirens began to wail. Even though Kaori had yelled out moments ago, she was instantly in front of us, a bo in her hand. Guards and ninjas ran up behind her.

"Get a move on!" I screamed to Hiro.

We tore around to the gate, but somehow Kaori got in front of us again. She jumped in our path, crouching and hissing. She snarled at me like a hungry lion. "You're not going anywhere," she said.

Guards were to the back of us. "I'll take them," Hiro said. "You deal with her." He ran off, fists flying. I heard grunts from the guards.

"Where did you get a bo?" I asked Kaori. The thing was almost as big as she was. I tried to grab it from her, but Kaori jumped back quickly, shaking her head. She raised the bo over her head, swirling it around in the air. Huh. Not too shabby.

I placed a kick to her side. She recoiled but kicked me right back. Her footwork was good—she hopped around fast.

Crack. The bo hit me on the shoulder, totally knocking

70

me for a loop. Kaori could *fight*! I ran up to her and grabbed her around her waist, planting my feet and flipping her over my head. She hit the ground with a grunt but rolled over quickly, scrambling to get her bo.

"Bring it on, bitch!" she screamed, waving her skinny arms around. "Or is that all you've got for me, Heaven Kogo?" She beat her chest with her bo and bent her knees. "You think it was fun bringing you back here? If I'd had my way, you would've died in Roppongi!"

I turned out my leg and kicked her right in the face. She spun backward, then bounced back. We whirled around for a while, kicking and punching, evenly matched. Every time I landed a punch to her stomach, she would batter me in the chest. I kicked her in the face; she flipped me over her shoulder.

I lay on the ground for a moment. She held the bo over her head, smiling sinisterly. "You're not going anywhere," she said again.

I saw a good opportunity to escape. I grabbed the bo, twisted my shoulders, rolled to the side, and brought her down. It surprised her. She landed hard on her back. It knocked the wind out of her. She gasped for breath and looked frantically at Masato's house. I brought the bo down, cracking it against her head, knocking her out.

I put my foot on her chest. I know, I know, totally *Gladiator*, but I'd been dying to do it. "That's for Roppongi," I said. She was out cold.

I folded up the bo and stuck it in my bag.

"Come on!" Hiro yelled, grabbing my hand. We went

through the front gate out to the street. The air raid sirens stopped. I looked back. Masato was nowhere to be seen. Had he even woken up? If he had, he was watching the whole ordeal from inside the house.

On the street I got a flash of something horrible surrounding Hiro. *Run,* my instincts said. *This isn't good.* So I started to run away from him as fast as I could.

"Wait, where are you going?" he shouted.

"I've changed my mind," I said over my shoulder. "I want you to stay away from me." Fighting Kaori had brought my confidence back. I was strong; I had a weapon now; I had a diamond necklace to sell. Maybe I could go to Kyoto and hide out in the Zen gardens. One thing was certain, though: I needed to stay away from Hiro. Seeing him in Japan, overhearing what those maids had said—even if it *wasn't* true— made him seem more dangerous than ever.

"No!" Hiro said, running after me. "I thought you said—"

"Don't you get it?" I said angrily, still running. "I don't trust you anymore, Hiro. I appreciate your chivalry in trying to rescue me. But as you can see, I got out of there just fine without you."

"Look, I realize how angry you are, and I know why," Hiro said, jogging alongside me. "I should have never lied to you about my ties to the yakuza. Which is why I didn't lie when you asked me if I hadn't for a moment considered accepting my father's offer."

"Well, it looks like you *did* accept it, didn't you?" I said smugly.

"No!" Hiro said. "I met with my father, yes. That was the

73

ruse to get back to Japan. Do you think I had money to get back here? He paid for my ticket. *He* picked me up at the airport. Or at least his driver did."

"Mr. Lumberman is all high and mighty now, huh?" I asked.

Hiro sighed. "I met with my father, but I haven't agreed to go through anything. And now I've escaped. I can never go back there again."

"Well, I can't forgive you!" I snapped. I stopped running and put my hands on my knees. I bent over, breathing heavily. Hiro stopped, too.

"Never?" he said. "I didn't want to lie to you. . . . I just . . . Does it mean anything, how far we've come together? Our loyalty to each other? If only in the samurai sense?"

"Don't bring that up right now," I said, remembering that one of the samurai tenets was to be loyal to your sensei. "All that stuff flew out the window when I found out you lied."

We were still in Masato's neighborhood. The street was deathly quiet. The trees cast ghostly shadows on the sidewalk. I looked up at a large high-rise apartment building. It was completely dark. Everyone was sound asleep.

Loyalty. I fumed. How dare Hiro play the samurai loyalty card?

"Listen, I want you to tell me everything you know," I said, hands on my hips. "Starting with why Masato didn't come out to get me back there. Why he didn't bring me back into the house. Why didn't he come out and drag me back in himself. Look at how easily we escaped! Those guards didn't even have guns!"

Hiro shook his head and looked down. "I don't know," he mumbled.

"He let me go!" I shouted. I looked up at the apartment building again. A light flicked on. I began to walk quickly down the sidewalk. Hiro followed me.

After a long pause—maybe too long—he continued. "I do know that Masato is keeping you under lock and key. They didn't want you running amok anymore. They . . ." He dropped his head.

"They *who*?" I said. "As in . . . Mieko?"

"Yes, her," Hiro said. He looked like he was searching for words.

Finally he spoke again. "I found out that Masato is just as entrenched in yakuza as your father is."

"How'd you find that out?"

"From . . . my father," he said, speaking very slowly. "He filled me in on some of the major participants in the organization. Like who is in the drug business, who runs the garbage rackets, who controls the gambling."

"This is making me sick," I spat.

"Masato is a big player," he continued.

"And your father?"

"My father is . . . yes. My father is too, now." He hung his head again. "But . . . but I'm not, Heaven! We are in the same danger and we should stick together."

"Funny, you sound like someone I know called Teddy," I said, and then realized—it was really true. Teddy had said those same words to me countless times. *We're in the same boat—we have to stick together.*

"Just trust me," Hiro said. "I realize that we can't be what we once were, but I still love you, and I want you safe." He took my hand.

My head hurt from when Masato had cracked it earlier today, and my body hurt from fighting Kaori. My lungs hurt from running. My heart hurt, too. I was lost.

"Well," I said, looking around. We were on another dark street. Down a ways was a gas station, eerily lit up but closed. It was as if we were the only people alive.

"This neighborhood creeps me out," I said. "Kaori's gonna send the dogs out to find us soon." I glared at him. "But one false move and I'm gone. You got that?"

Hiro paused for a moment. He swallowed ever so softly. But I heard it.

"Of course," he said, regaining his voice. I narrowed my eyes at him, then spun on my heel and started walking.

"This way," Hiro said. We passed a trashy-looking geisha girl in fishnets and hot pants.

I was disoriented. Hiro had insisted that he knew a "shortcut," but we'd been walking for hours. The neighborhood we'd just entered looked seedy. Were we near Shinjuku? It *seemed* like it, I thought.

I looked at a storefront in front of us. KABUKICHO KARAOKE. Outside were a couple of broken pachinko machines. And then a heap of what looked like pachinko-machine parts. In the next storefront I looked right in and saw a bunch of shady-looking suits in stained, sleeveless shirts huddled around a table. A taller guy in a velour tracksuit rolled some dice. They all shouted when the dice hit the table, and I cowered back.

"We're in *Kabukicho*?" I hissed to Hiro.

This was the land of the yakuza.

"What are we doing here?" I said, starting to panic. My body bristled. *This is a bad move, this is a bad move, this is a bad move,* said my brain. I glanced at the street. Crack pipes, bottles, used condoms, and cigarette butts littered the gutter.

"We had to go this way in order *not* to go by my father's neighborhood," Hiro said. He looked me over quickly and took off his bulky sweatshirt.

"Here, put this on and pull up the hood," he said. "Hurry."

"There were five million other ways we could've gone," I argued, stopping in my tracks. A burly guy pushed past me. I drew the cords on the hood tight. "Why are we doing this?"

"Just a circuitous route. Trust me. Let's just get through here quick," Hiro said, taking my hand and dragging me down an alley. I heard angry voices coming from somewhere.

An uneasy feeling crept over me. Was this . . . was this a trap?

A thuggish guy came up to us, his hair in a tightly coiled perm. He had squinty little eyes and a piggish face and was about three times Hiro's size. My heart started to pound. He was staring right at us.

"What are you doing here?" he said. At first I thought he was talking to me. I opened my mouth to answer.

"Hey, man," Hiro said, shaking his hand.

I clamped my mouth shut. *Hiro* knew this guy? He was missing a part of his little finger. I could see the outline of a gun in his pants. Across the street a guy and a girl, arm in arm, came out of a seedy-looking bar. The girl had on an ugly gray-and-white fur stole and tottered on four-inch heels. All of a sudden she screamed, picked up a stray bottle, and threw it at the boyfriend. The guy let out a grunt and lunged at her and started punching her again and again. No one tried to stop them. I looked away.

"Yo," the guy answered, barely noticing what was happening.

"Uh . . . Suki, this is Aki." He turned to me. Apparently for the moment my name was Suki.

"Hey," Aki said, barely looking at me, not shaking my hand. I wondered—with my freaky, grown-out, black-roots-showing geisha hair and my skimpy sleeping outfit and my skater-boy hoodie—maybe he thought I was a hooker. Either that or a homeless waif named Suki.

"So you know where we can get a car?" Hiro said. "I'd like to take a little drive."

I was fuming. He was asking *this* meathead? The car was obviously going to be hot.

"Yeah, I'm not on that shit anymore," Aki said, leaning down. "He's got me on the H tip now. That and crystal meth." He smiled. All of his teeth were crooked. "But hey, congrats on the ceremony tomorrow."

Hiro bristled. "Ah, it's been postponed," he said in a low voice.

"What's been postponed?" I said.

Both of the guys looked at me, and I could tell that Aki suddenly recognized who I was. He did a double take, then looked back at Hiro.

"Maybe you wanna ask someone else in the neighborhood, though," Aki said. "About the car, I mean." His gaze wandered back to me. He squinted, as if asking himself, *Is that Heaven Kogo? Or is it just Suki the hooker?*

I quickly pretended I was very interested in the bar we were standing in front of. I peeked inside. Skanky girls danced naked on the stage. They looked about thirteen years old.

"Okay, thanks," Hiro was saying. He grabbed my hand. "See you around."

"No doubt," Aki said.

I grabbed his arm, hard. "Who was that?" I asked.

Hiro sucked in air uncomfortably. "He works for your father," he said. "I don't think he recognized you, though."

Chills ran up and down my spine.

"What was he talking about, the ceremony?" I asked.

Hiro didn't answer. He navigated through the dark streets. We nearly bumped into two guys with tattooed arms and legs, sitting on the bottom step of a building, busily snorting something off a mirror. Right in plain view. A skinny girl sat beside them, swinging her legs, wearing nothing but a tiny bra and underpants. She looked my age. When they finished with the mirror, they passed it over to her.

We walked by an alley where a businessman in a suit and tie was getting beat up by two bald muscleheads. The only word I could hear them grunt was *money*. Hiro tried to hide the sight from me, but I'd already seen the worst. The guy's face was a pulpy, horrible mess. They were no doubt going to kill him.

"Come on," Hiro said.

I felt worse and worse with every step. *This is wrong,* I told myself. *All of this. Hiro, everything.* Every guy that passed, I wondered, *Does he work for my father? Does he work for Teddy's father? Does he work for Masato?*

Do any of these guys work for Hiro's father?

What was even creepier was that when we passed by a group of guys, one of them turned and patted Hiro on the back. "Hey, man," he said. The others nodded at him. In another cluster Hiro got another nod. They *knew* him. But he'd only been back for a few days. What was going *on?*

"How do they all *know* you?" I whispered.

I felt like I was in free fall.

And then I realized what I wanted. How desperate I was. I stopped. "I need to see my father," I said.

"What?" Hiro said, turning around slowly.

"Get me out of here. I want to see my father. Now." I narrowed my eyes at him.

"Heaven, you can't—" he said.

"Why is everyone *saying* that I can't see him? What are you talking about? Why can't I?" I felt like I was in jail. Like I couldn't breathe.

I tried to stare him down. "What do you *know?*"

Hiro didn't say anything.

"Why did we just have to walk through there? Were

you . . . were you just passing a code to some other yakuza guy? Why can't I see my father? What's going on?"

"You're imagining things," he said. "There was no secret code."

He's like the rest of them, I thought. *Just like Masato and all the others.*

"You just can't see him," he said. "I . . ."

Guys rushed past us, nodding to Hiro.

"I want to see my father," I said again, slowly and angrily.

"I'm sorry," Hiro said. He looked distracted and nervous. He glanced at his watch. "I can't let you do that."

There was something behind his eyes that looked . . . I don't know. Untrustworthy. Wrong, somehow.

"Fine," I said. I turned and began to run. My footsteps rang out on the sidewalk under me. I dodged a bunch of guys hanging around, smoking a joint. I ran through a swarm of hookers and disgusting-looking guys. I ran and ran and ran and realized I had no idea where I was. I had no idea where the hell my father was, either. I turned a corner and fought back tears. Shit. I was in front of KABUKICHO KARAOKE again. I windmilled around, wondering how I'd gone in a circle.

I was lost in my own damn city.

I stopped and put my arms out in the ready stance, prepared to kick someone's ass if they came near. Including Hiro. I had to make a plan.

"Heaven," said a voice.

I turned. There he was.

"Get away," I snarled.

"Look, I don't know where he is, okay?"

"Liar."

"All right . . ." He put his head down. "I know where he is, but there's no way you could get to him. Not now." He looked up at me finally. His eyes looked remorseful and pained. I gritted my teeth. I *hated* him. I'd never been so filled with hate for anyone before in my life.

"They'll kill you if you try to get to him," he said.

There was conviction in his voice. He was telling the truth.

I looked down at the ground. It was littered with huge shards of broken glass. I heard a police siren in the distance.

"I can get you out of here," Hiro said quietly. "You just have to trust me."

"I *don't* trust you," I said, biting back tears. "I'm terrified of you."

"But you shouldn't be," he said. He tried to come closer, but I backed away.

"What an ass you are, leading me through Kabukicho like that. How *stupid* are you?" I said. I blinked. Now I *was* crying. "You know, it hurt to find out my father was in the yakuza. It hurt to find out that Mieko would rather I was dead. It hurt to find out that Kaori wanted to kill me, and it hurt to find out that everything that came out of Masato's mouth was a lie. These are people who said, 'You'll be safe with us, Heaven,' and then they turn me around and stab me in the back. But you know. . . ." I sniffed and wiped my face. They were angry tears. My blood boiled hot. "I can *deal* with all of them. I knew I shouldn't trust any of them, anyway. But *you*." I pointed my finger at him. "To realize that *you* are deceiving me . . . that's a different story."

He didn't say a word. I glared at him. I wished that I just didn't care. I wished that I could just walk away and leave Hiro and put all of this behind me. But I stood there, so angry I was shaking.

"Please," he said. "I'm not deceiving you." His voice was desperate and pleading. "How can I get you to believe me?"

He paused. "Kabukicho was a mistake. I'm sorry. I thought we could get a car. Again, *I'm sorry.*"

He swallowed. "But I can't let you go see your father. I know this for sure. Just *believe me* on this one. If you try to see your father, you'll die."

"Just tell me where he is," I said quietly.

"But then you'll go. . . ."

"I *won't* go, all right?" I said. "Just treat me with enough respect to tell me at least where he *is*."

Hiro paused. He rubbed his hands together. He moved his foot, raking it against the broken glass.

"He's at your house," he said. "But he's . . . he's near death."

Then in a lower voice he said, "They're killing him."

My chin quivered.

We didn't say anything for a moment. I tried to keep it together.

"Look at me," he said. He walked a little closer. I didn't move away.

"Heaven, look at me. Please. I love you. I'm trying to take care of you. I'm trying to keep you safe. I'm loyal to you. We went through that neighborhood because that would be the *last* place anyone would look. But this was a mistake. And I'm sorry. But really. I'm going to *get you out of here*. Do you understand?"

I thought of my father, on life support, in our house. They were killing him. That sense I'd had—back at Masato's—had been right. Rage bubbled up inside me. I wanted to tear Masato limb from limb. I looked at Hiro, now completely overwhelmed with emotion.

"Will you help me get out of Japan?" I asked.

He nodded. "Yes. Of course. That's what I was thinking, too. Out of Japan."

I paused. There was a chance I'd never see my father again. I was powerless. How could I stop this? How could I reverse this without putting myself in danger?

No, I had to leave. Now.

"All right," I said. "Help me get out of Japan."

Relief flooded his eyes. "Thank you," he said, wrapping his arms around me. I stayed stiff as a board and didn't hug him back.

He grabbed my hand. "This way." We were in full-fledged Shinjuku now. The place was still hopping, even though it had to be about 3 A.M. Hiro flagged down a cab. It stopped right in front of an Irish pub–type bar; a girl was throwing up in the alleyway. "Get in!" he yelled at me.

I stood around the flashing lights. They sort of looked like the EKG machines you see in hospitals.

They're killing him.

I looked up at the sky. I would have to say good-bye to my father here, at least for now. I closed my eyes. "Try to hold on," I whispered to him.

"Heaven, get in!" Hiro cried.

I turned back to him. What could I do? Stand around Shinjuku all night? So I climbed into the car and tried to clear my mind, if only for a moment.

6

The cab zipped around the corner. The driver craned his neck around to look at us. "Where are you going?"

I looked at Hiro, my eyebrows raised in question.

"I know someone who can help us get out of the country," Hiro said, his voice still quivering. "She can get us back to the States."

"We're going back to the *States?*"

Hiro muttered something to the driver in a quiet voice that I couldn't hear. I gripped the side of the car. The cab-driver jerked the car forward, driving out of Shinjuku, nearly running over a line of drunk teenage tourists who were staggering across the street.

"Hold up. What did you tell him?" I said angrily.

He took my hands. "There's something important I have to tell you. A reason why I might be able to help. *And* the reason why you should go back to the States."

The cab jerked to a nauseating halt. "Look, I don't know if I want to go back with—"

"It's your mother. Your . . . your *birth* mother."

My head shot up.

He nodded. "I've found something out. I couldn't tell you back there on Masato's property, but . . . I think I know where she is."

"My *birth* mother?" I said. My voice was raw. Suddenly my palms went slick with sweat. What was he talking about? "What do you . . . ?"

The cab turned a corner, taking us out of Shinjuku. The sun was just beginning to climb in the sky. The terrain looked gorgeous—green and peaceful.

My *birth mother*? Was Hiro on *crack*? Was this a trap?

Hiro cleared his throat. "I found some documents in my father's desk. I don't know how he got ahold of them, but perhaps he got them from Yoji Yukemura since he . . . uh . . . works for him now. Or maybe Yoji got them from your father somehow; I don't know. It could be a bribe or something.

"But anyway, it's information about *you*. Or rather, about your birth mother. The information was very cryptic, and there wasn't a name, just 'female,' living in the San Diego area, with a certain amount of money next to her name."

"San Diego?" I croaked. "Are you sure?"

Hiro grabbed my hand. "We can go and find her," he said. "Isn't this something you've always wondered about?"

"Yes, of course," I said, a little snappishly. "But how do

you know this isn't, like, a setup or something?" My heart beat quickly. My birth mother. In San Diego all this time, and I had no idea. I could have gone to *her* instead. . . .

Hiro looked me in the eye. "I'm not lying to you. I can see you're skeptical. But really, I'm not making this up." His expression got very cryptic. "My father confirmed it as well."

"He *did*?" How did all of Tokyo know about my birth mother except me?

"Yes," Hiro said. "Now will you let me help you?"

I quivered. "Why didn't you tell me this sooner?" I asked. I didn't know whether to be angry or excited. I was still pumped from our standoff in Kabukicho. My legs were still shaking.

"Because . . ." Hiro stopped. "We needed to be somewhere quieter. Not on the street. Not running." He waved his hand around him, indicating that the cab was somewhere "quieter." Up front the driver yammered on his cell phone and continued to drive in a jerky, stop-start fashion. A pine-scented tree hung from his rearview mirror, but the air smelled more like sweat than pine.

"Wow," I said. "I'm having a little trouble believing this."

"Well, believe it," Hiro said. He took my hand. It felt warm, just as I remembered. I was about to pull away, but the hand felt comforting. My pulse began to race again.

"So you see?" he went on. "Doesn't the States make sense now?"

"Yeah," I said. "But how do we know she *wants* me to find her?"

"She will," Hiro said. His eyes glazed over with what looked like love. I swallowed hard.

"I had an idea yesterday of how we could get out of the country," he said after a little while. "Yokosuka U.S. Navy Base. I know someone who can help us there. That's where I told the cabdriver to go. It's about seventy miles from here."

"The U.S. *Navy*?" I repeated. "As in aircraft carriers and people doing a lot of marching and chanting and . . . and bazookas?"

"I know someone who might be able to smuggle us on a boat back to San Diego. It'll be dangerous, because they'll have to sneak us on the boat and then into the country. But I know someone who might take that risk. Hopefully she won't have shipped out somewhere else by now."

"She?" My eyebrows raised.

"Yes, a friend from home."

"If only we could do something normal, like take a commercial plane," I murmured. "JAL, back to San Diego."

"No planes," Hiro said softly.

"Yeah, I know."

It was our old banter. Then I remembered. My world was upside down. I had a *birth mother* who was alive. And Hiro knew every yakuza thug in Kabukicho.

The cab sped through the dark streets of Tokyo, heading for points north, an old kabuki theater broadcast quietly playing on the radio. I settled back into the seat. The clanging kabuki drums made my head ring. Hiro's hand still rested on top of mine, warm and comforting. I didn't know if I wanted to pull my hand away or not.

Soon we were driving along miles and miles of coastline. Hiro and I had settled into a silence. My hand now rested on my lap, and Hiro kept his hands to himself. I stole a quick glance at him.

What was going on in his mind? I had to believe he was telling the truth about my mother. I snuck another look at him. His jawline was so sexy.

I flinched.

And then it hit me. I wasn't over this guy. I still had feelings for him. Despite not trusting him. Despite hating him. Despite everything.

We rolled up to what I guessed was the navy base entrance. Two Americans sat in a little hut at the front. One of them came out of the gate. *Whoa,* I thought. *That's quite an Uzi slung around his back.*

"I thought this was peacetime," I muttered.

Hiro got out of the car and started talking to the guy. The driver grumbled in the front, unsure of where we were. I realized how dumb this was. Why would this guy let us inside? Weren't military bases like super-secure?

They allowed Hiro inside the little hut; he picked up a telephone and started to speak into it. I shifted in my seat, thinking. There had been a moment back there when I'd seriously thought Hiro was in on a plot to kill me or something. Why had I thought that? Was it just paranoia?

I wondered briefly what Masato was doing. Was Tokyo

under lockdown, looking for me? Were those air raid sirens sounding again?

Did my birth mother *really* live in San Diego?

I looked around. I could smell the ocean, but I couldn't see it. The only things visible were the little huts. A concrete path extended past the huts but disappeared into the trees. To my right and left was scrubby grass and shrubs. A sign that said No Trespassing. No snipers at treetops, guns poised. Just that one buzz-cut, skinny kid with the Uzi and the other guy in the hut.

Hiro came back to the car and stuck his head in the window. "We're in."

"You're kidding," I said.

Hiro explained that he'd called his friend, Melissa Martin, who was stationed here but originally from L.A. She could be our ticket out of Japan. Hiro handed the cabby some money and he drove away. We stood in front of the hut, apparently waiting for something.

"So . . . is she coming to get us?" I asked. The Uzi guy glared at me.

"Yes," Hiro said, not making eye contact.

"Are we leaving today?" I whispered.

"Shhh," Hiro said. The Uzi guy sighed loudly.

A dusty jeep rolled up to the entrance. Driving was a tiny girl in a tan uniform. She waved at Hiro. He waved back. Hiro pulled on my arm and led me to the backseat. He nudged me to climb in. The car had barely stopped. Then quickly he himself went around to the front seat. Jeep girl pulled him over to her side, let out a little squeal, and gave him a gigantic hug.

91

Whoa.

She broke away and turned to the guards. "I'll take them from here, Kyle," she said loudly in a tough voice to the Uzi guy. He nodded, scowling now.

"Where are we going?" I asked cautiously.

"Getting you out of sight," she said in a rushed, no-nonsense tone. She glanced at me briefly. "I'm Melissa."

She looked a little like an elf—she couldn't have been more than five-foot two. Her nose, cheeks, ears, and hands were tiny. Her hair was long, blond, and curly and draped down her back. But even though she was small, she drove crazily. Way too fast, taking turns quickly and dangerously.

"So we need to get out of here as soon as possible," Hiro said. "I know that this isn't something you normally do, but if there's any chance . . ."

Melissa wrinkled her nose. "I could get dishonorably discharged. I could lose my college fund. At the very least I could be demoted and fined." She smiled a tight smile.

I raised my eyebrow, in the backseat.

"But for you," Melissa said, her hand now on Hiro's knee, "I'll do this."

"Thanks," Hiro said.

Interesting.

Melissa's eyes flickered briefly to me in the rearview mirror. Then they settled back on Hiro. "Are you wanted by the police?"

He grimaced. "Not exactly."

"Care to explain?"

"I . . . I can't," Hiro said. He twiddled his thumbs q..
habit he had when he was nervous. "I mean, you know. . . ."

"Yeah, sure. Same old danger," Melissa said after a
tense pause. I wondered how much she knew about Hiro's
past.

She took a sharp turn, nearly tipping over the jeep. "I
know one guy who will sneak you on board. But he won't be
on the sub himself. You're going to have to stay hidden. I
can also provide you with some food. The trip will take
about four days. I can get you water at least. Probably
more. Granola bars, maybe. Cereal."

"Hold up," I said. "Did you say *sub*? As in *submarine*?"

"Yeah," Melissa huffed. Hiro turned back to me, his
mouth a straight line, his eyes cautious.

"I was thinking we'd go on a boat or something," I said
quietly. "Like, you know, aboveground."

"You want to be incognito," Melissa said, her voice
angry. "How could you be incognito on a ship? Were you
thinking like a sailboat or something?"

"Jeez, settle down," I whispered.

"It makes the most sense," Hiro said.

I sighed. "All right," I said. I had to remember why we
were going. My *mother*.

We pulled into a parking lot that was in front of a long,
one-story building. Next to it was a basketball court.
Melissa jumped out of the jeep. Hiro followed. I crawled out
slowly, feeling dizzy. I hadn't eaten in a million years. As
soon as my feet hit the ground, my knees buckled, and my
vision went spotty.

"Whoa," I heard Hiro say. Then I felt strong hands under my armpits hoisting me back up. I struggled to open my eyes. I thought it was Hiro lifting me, but it turned out to be Melissa. She was *strong*.

"Low blood sugar," Melissa said to Hiro. My body felt hot, then cold. "She needs to eat something."

Hiro ran over and held me around my waist. Melissa fetched something from her jeep. She put it to my lips. It was a can of Coke. I let the warm liquid run down my throat. I felt a little better and stood up straight.

"I can make you something in my apartment," Melissa said. She looked right and left. The place was deserted. The parking lot was full of jeeps; the basketball court off to the side of the building was empty. Then again, it was only five-thirty on a Sunday morning.

"Come on," Melissa said, taking Hiro's arm. "Before anyone sees us."

We quickly ran into the squat building and walked halfway down a long corridor. The place was dark and depressing. "The sub deploys in about six hours," Melissa whispered to us over her shoulder. "I know that Andy will help sneak you guys on, and he can contact someone in San Diego to get you off, but I think you'll be on your own after that."

"What did you tell the guards?" I asked. "Won't they come looking for us?"

"The guards and I have an understanding," Melissa said brusquely.

She unlocked the door to her suite and ushered us inside. "We shouldn't turn on many lights," she said. She snapped on a tiny light over the stove and stuck her head into the fridge. I walked around the apartment. The interior was about as drab and uninspired as the outside. Standard-issue couch, coffee table, a radio sitting on a cardboard box, a pile of what looked like workout clothes in the corner. Through an open door I saw her bed, rumpled and unmade. I sat down tentatively on the couch, trying to adjust my eyes to the dim blue light.

Melissa quickly started cracking eggs. The smell of them at first made me woozy, but then I realized I was starving. While Hiro was in the bathroom, I fidgeted. I didn't know what to say. She seemed so standoffish. It was almost as if Hiro hadn't told her on the phone at the gate that there would be someone with him. It seemed also that maybe they'd had something once.

"So how do you know Hiro?" I asked, my voice coming out creaky and small.

"Here." She walked over and handed me a large glass of orange juice. I gratefully drank it.

"Hiro helped me back in L.A.," she said, turning back to the stove.

"Really?" I said. "You're from L.A.?" I tried to figure out how old she was. She couldn't have been more than eighteen or nineteen.

"Yeah," she said gruffly. "I was dating someone who was totally bad news. He was in a gang—real trouble. Then he started stalking me. He'd make these really awful phone calls to my house and follow me around everywhere. It got to be totally creepy."

95

She stuck two slices of bread in the toaster. "At one point he cornered me. He had a knife. Luckily, I'd just hung out with Hiro. He'd sensed something wrong with the situation and wasn't far from my house. When he heard me scream, he came running back."

"It wasn't really like that," Hiro said, walking in from the bathroom.

"You're too modest," Melissa said, giving him a majorly flirty push. "After that kind of fright, I decided to join the military. Get strong. Protect myself. A little extreme, I know, but I wanted to be in control of my situation. Plus I give four years to the navy and they're gonna let me go to college for free."

I shot Hiro a suspicious look. How long could this have been before *my* wedding, before I'd showed up on his doorstep? Was he saving damsels in distress left and right?

God, I was catty. I was trying my hardest to *not* be in love with Hiro. Melissa handed me a plate of eggs, toast, and sausage. I thanked her, but she'd already turned back to Hiro. I took a huge bite of the eggs and closed my eyes. It felt so good to *eat*. I started shoveling everything else in quickly. Melissa glanced at me and wrinkled her nose.

"Where have you traveled so far?" Hiro asked in a quiet voice.

"All over," Melissa said. "Russia, Kuwait, all over the Mediterranean. They love selling the navy people rugs in some of those Middle Eastern countries."

"Rugs?"

"Yeah. Weird, huh? But they're handmade."

"You're looking well," Hiro said as he spooned some eggs onto his plate.

"Yeah, this has been good for me," she said firmly, taking a large, crackly bite out of her toast.

Then there was a knock on the door. We froze.

Melissa glared at us. "Into the bedroom," she whispered. "Quick. Hide."

Hiro and I scurried into the bedroom and dove under her bed. I got a mouthful of dust and tried my hardest not to sneeze.

"She's friendly," I whispered to Hiro in a sarcastic tone of voice.

"At least she's helping us," Hiro hissed.

From my spot under the bed I had a good view of Melissa's foyer. I watched as she quickly put our plates in the fridge and walked over to open the door. Light flooded in. It was the Uzi guy from the front gate. He looked over Melissa's shoulder into the room. "Those people who are visiting you," he said. "Where are they?"

"They're walking around the grounds, Kyle," Melissa said casually. "I told them I was tired and we'd get breakfast later."

A pause. I held my breath. Some agreement she had with the front guards.

"What's that on the counter?" he boomed.

"I got hungry," Melissa said. "Did a lot of running yesterday."

A silence lasted for a minute or so.

"All right," the Uzi guy finally said. "I got a call from the captain saying no visitors today. Probably because of the launch. So when they get back, you'll have to escort them out, okay?"

"Of course," Melissa said. "No problem."

I saw the guy look around the room once more. Then she shut the door behind him and walked into the bedroom. "Hey," she whispered after a few moments. "He's gone. You can come out."

I crawled out; dust bunnies were stuck to my legs.

"We gotta get you on that sub now," Melissa said. "I need to contact Andy quickly."

"Who's Andy?" Hiro inquired.

"Well, let's just say that he and I go way back," she replied slyly.

"Is that so?" Hiro replied.

Why was he taking such an interest in this?

"If you must know, he asked me to marry him a while back and I told him I couldn't. I was still getting over someone else," she said while staring deeply into Hiro's eyes.

"Can we trust him?" I asked, trying to get her to stop gazing at Hiro.

"He's the only one who'll be able to get you out of here in one piece," Melissa said, walking back to the kitchen. She stuck her head in the fridge again and pulled out a big jug of distilled water. "You're going to need some supplies," she said, shoving it at me.

She pulled down a box of cereal and a jar of peanut butter. "Here. This will keep you alive for four days, at least."

Then we hustled out of her room and ducked down the narrow corridor. Hiro and I walked quickly behind, a little dazed. Melissa approached a door at the end of the hall and started to pound on it.

After about twenty angry knocks with her fist, a tousle-headed, sleepy-looking guy in boxers and a T-shirt hung in the doorway. "What?" he said.

"Good, you're up," Melissa said. "We need access to the sub."

Andy groaned. "God, *why*?" he said. Then he glanced at us: me with the box of cereal and peanut butter, Hiro with the jug of water. He rolled his eyes. "You know the sub isn't leaving for about six hours."

"I know," Melissa said. "But these two need to disappear. *Now.*"

He shut the door briefly. Hiro squeezed my hand. I could hear Andy bumping around in his room, opening and shutting drawers. In about two minutes he emerged, dressed in a T-shirt that said Annapolis and frayed camouflage cargo pants.

"Let's go," he said, brushing by us. Hiro nudged me forward.

Andy led us out the side door, around to the back of the building, through brushy grass to a dirt path, and through a bunch of bushes and dunes. We climbed over the hills, our shoes sinking into the sand. This seemed to take forever. The jumbo jar of peanut butter weighed a million pounds. The diamond necklace in my bag kept slapping against my thigh; I was sure I'd have a bruise. Then we climbed the largest dune and suddenly there was a clearing. My legs ached; I leaned over to stretch. We all peeked out from the trees and saw, over the hill, a pavilion of more brown, squat buildings. And beyond that a long, wide concrete dock. Beyond that the Sea of Japan, gray and choppy.

I could see the sub. The top of it poked through the water. It was oily and black and looked like a giant torpedo.

I shivered. It looked like a mirage.

"We gotta get around those guards," Andy said in a low voice, pointing at what looked like a guard shack at the end of the dock. "Melissa, you have to distract them. I'll get these two on and show them where to go."

"Is this a regular operation for you two?" I said, half joking.

Everyone ignored me. I shivered again.

Melissa turned to Hiro. "So this might be the last time I see you," she said. "Andy's gonna get you on the sub if everything goes as planned. I won't be able to get on board to say good-bye."

"Well . . . ," Hiro said, grasping for words. "I don't know how to thank you. . . ."

"What will happen if we're detected?" I interrupted. The wind blew through my T-shirt. I wished I'd worn something a little more substantial.

"Worst-case scenario, you'll be shot," Melissa said blandly, her eyes still on Hiro. "Which is why you have to follow Andy's every instruction." She glanced at me, her eyes narrowed, as if she was certain I was going to screw up. I squared my shoulders and tensed. I was glad we were getting away from Melissa. If we hadn't been leaving right this minute, I might have had to kick her ass for good measure.

Melissa turned to Hiro. "So," she said, wiping her hands on her pants, brushing the hair out of her face. "It sucks that we only got to see each other for a couple of minutes."

"Yeah," Hiro said. "It would've been better if we'd caught up on . . . less dangerous terms."

"Oh, well," Melissa said, turning her gruff voice into a syrupy-sweet, flirtatious one. "Hopefully some other time . . . soon . . ."

And then in one big burst of momentum she wrapped herself around Hiro. She buried her head in his neck, almost as if she were crying. But to my shock she lifted her head, glanced at me out of the corner of her eye, and *kissed him on the lips*. Long and hard. Openmouthed.

I backed up.

"Will you be all right?" Hiro said, pulling away slightly, seeming a little shaken from the kiss.

Melissa stood back. "Yeah, I'll be fine."

"Well, thank you," Hiro said. "I really owe you one."

"Yes, thank you," I said, the words coming out garbled and unintelligible.

"If you change your mind," Melissa said, "call me. We can get you back on the base, I think."

She was clearly saying this only to Hiro.

And then she quickly turned and dashed down the hill, her heels lifted high. She slowed and walked over to the guard booth, which looked quite a lot like the one at the entrance to the base. I squinted. There were three guards, all sitting down. They wore high black boots and machine guns on their backs. At the top of one of the higher buildings was a spinning satellite, blinking angrily. But aside from this activity, the place was deserted and weird. It felt like what a beach must have been like right before some massive World War II battle. Quiet, but eerie. It didn't feel peaceful in the least.

The wind whipped through me. Hiro reached for my hand, but I pulled it away, thinking of Melissa kissing him on the mouth. It gave me a sour feeling in my stomach.

Andy squinted at the group of guards. Melissa had approached them. Now they were talking.

"Okay, we're going to run down this hill quickly," he growled to us. "Follow me. Stay down. Like she said, if they see us, they might shoot at us. So keep low.

"Then we'll have to wade under the dock for part of the way. Right until we get to the base of the sub. Then we'll climb up to the hatch and go in. You got that?"

I nodded, frozen, and took a deep breath. Beside me, Hiro was also readying himself.

And then in a dizzying instant we dashed down the dune, staying low to the ground. My feet sank farther and farther into the sand. We reached the water's edge and plunged in. I held my bag and the cereal above my head so they wouldn't get wet.

The water was murky and cold, but at least the waves weren't big. We waded out to the sub, Andy looking behind at us angrily. "Faster!" he said.

We reached the base of the sub and climbed up the ladder to the hatch. Andy opened the hatch—a huge metal door—and waved us both in. "Come on, come on, dammit!" he said, quiet so his voice wouldn't be picked up in the wind. "You're too slow!"

"Oof," I muttered, somehow stubbing my toe as I climbed down the ladder, which was slippery to hold. This was all happening too quickly. I glanced for an instant at the shoreline. Melissa was still talking to the guards. She had their backs to the ocean. No one had seen us. The dunes rose in back of them, pale and silent.

"Get down!" Andy said.

As soon as I stepped off the ladder, I realized we were in a cylindrical shaft. The lights were fluorescent and unattractive. There was a blank TV screen and what looked like a CB radio. There was also a regular-looking radio, but it wasn't switched on. I didn't smell the ocean. I could only smell something like Clorox. The little room was spotless.

Andy bent down and started twisting a huge dial on the floor to the left. He used all of his strength to push it, then began to pull straight up. Hiro tried to help, but Andy shooed him away. Finally the dial and the floor lifted up. It was another hatch. Once the door was open, I peered down below. Another ladder.

"Come on," he said. He started to climb down.

Hiro and I carefully made our way down. To my right and left were huge hoselike contraptions, dials, pulleys, pipes.

I hit the floor and turned. There was a long hallway of wooden doors. Andy was quickly walking away from us. We wound around more corridors of ropes, hoses, ladders (there must have been an upper deck), and pulleys until we came into a wider space, with lots of padded tables. I looked left. There were ovens, what looked like a griddle, and big chrome refrigerators.

"Mess deck," Andy said, slapping one of the tables. "Not that you'll be eating here or anything."

I spied a loaf of bread, all wrapped up, sitting on the counter. Peanut butter would taste better with bread. But I felt like if I made one false move, Andy would come over and strangle me.

Again we sped through another corridor. Strange noises creaked from somewhere in the sub. I glanced back at Hiro. In the fluorescent light he looked uncomfortable. I wondered if he was thinking about Melissa. Was she still talking to the guards?

We passed a bunch of small wooden doors. "The crew berths," Andy said dryly. "We're almost there." He walked up to the end door on the corridor, next to a hatch that said, DO NOT ENTER WITHOUT CLEARANCE. Rifling through his pocket, he brought out a set of keys and unlocked the room.

"Here," he grunted. He shoved open the door, and there was our room.

I looked at Hiro. There seemed to be something off about him. Was this a bad idea? I felt butterflies in my stomach.

Andy stood at the door, beckoning us to go through. "Come on," he said, irritated. "In you go."

So we stepped inside.

I remember every minute of the two dates Hiro and I had back in L.A. I recorded them in my journal to make sure I wouldn't forget. To me, we just felt so right together. So perfect. And I knew in my heart that Hiro someday would realize it, too. I just had to wait for him.

And now he calls at about 5 A.M., and I still think I'm dreaming, but then I'm driving to meet him, and there he is. . . .

That kiss we shared. God . . .

But then there's this girl with him. This ragtag, pouty girl who looks like she's been crying, who's scared shitless. Who knows where he found her! I know all about Hiro. Not that he ever told me much about himself, but I know the kind of world he comes from. I had an idea when I was in L.A., but when I came to Japan, I heard a lot of underground whisperings about Hiro's family and the kind of stuff he's connected to.

But still. Girl or no girl. She probably won't last long with him. He'll realize soon that he should be back with me. I know I shouldn't, but I'm hoping something goes wrong on the sub. It's amazing they even got on safely. I practically had to take my top off to distract those guards. After Andy came back, we slunk away quickly. It's awkward between us now, but luckily he has no idea that Hiro is the person I still have feelings for. Then I tracked down Mark, who is going to be the sub's cook. I found him in the gym, doing bicep curls on a bench. We've fooled around a little, me and Mark. I know I can trust him.

"Listen," I said in a low voice. "There's a boy who's stowing away on the sub. Now, if nothing happens, you don't know anything about him. He's going to stay out of sight.

But if something does happen and you guys need to evacuate, I want you to make sure he gets out okay."

Mark nodded. "But I don't know anything else about it," he said. "If I hear him, I'm reporting it."

"Fine," I said. "Just help me out if something happens to the sub."

Mark agreed.

"He's the only person I know will be stowing away," I said. "You don't need to be responsible for anyone else who's on board."

"Is there someone else?" Mark asked, eyebrows raised.

"No," I said. "Not that I know of. Just him."

Someday Hiro will realize I'm the only girl for him. He'll come back.

I should probably be worried about that jackass Kyle from the front gate coming back and looking for Hiro and that Heaven girl. But they've probably already forgotten about it. They've switched shifts by now anyway. It's not like we wrote their names in the book or anything. Besides, I'm outta here soon. They're gonna be sending us off to the demilitarized zone up on the North Korea–South Korea border. I should be worried about staying alive. But now, with the image and smell of Hiro fresh in my mind, I have something to live for.

The phone rings and scares me out of my mind. Could it be the gate, wondering where those two are? I pick up.

There's heavy breathing on the other end. Sounds far away. Traffic noises are in the background.

"Hello?" I say.

"I hear you had some visitors," the caller says. It's a guy.

The voice sounds absolutely possessed. Could this be someone playing a joke on me?

"Ha, very funny," I say.

"There's nothing funny about it," the voice continues.

I feel a chill that cools me right down to the soles of my feet.

"Tell me where they've gone, or torture awaits you," the voice says calmly. "Torture beyond your wildest dreams. Think military torture is bad? Think POW torture is bad? This is ten million times worse."

I bite my lip. How can this be possible? I quiver, ready to hang up. But the voice speaks again.

"We can see you right now," the voice says. "We know where you are."

I believe them. I can't speak.

Finally I swallow hard and close my eyes. "San Diego," I say.

"Good girl," the voice says. Then I hear a dial tone.

I sit on my bed. My whole body shakes. Then I realize. The voice I heard on the other end—it wasn't a man's, as I'd first thought. It was a woman's. And it was the scariest voice I'd ever heard.

Melissa

7

Andy explained that the sub wouldn't be fully occupied; otherwise this bunk room would have been reserved for the crew. "This is, however, the smallest bunk room," he explained. "The others are slightly larger. But you guys are damn lucky you've even got that. I don't know where else we would've put you."

I looked around. It was a fluorescent-lit box that was about as big as the inside of a Mini Cooper. The walls were painted a weird sea foam green, and everything—the chrome of the beds, the blue curtains, the wood panels, the cement floors—was absolutely spotless.

"The problem is that this room is right next to the other crew quarters," Andy said. "Those doors we passed? All crew bunks. Therefore, you have to lock this from the inside and *keep the lights off.* If you turn them on, they'll wonder what's up and unlock this from the outside. But if you keep quiet—and I mean *quiet*—I think you should be okay. It's only a four-day run."

He snapped the lights off. We fell into darkness. I could hear everyone's breathing, it was so quiet. "You're going to have to get used to the light like this. Either of you got a penlight?"

"I do," Hiro said. I heard him rustling around in his pockets.

"You can use that. But nothing else."

"What about a bathroom?" I asked.

Andy snickered. "Well, I'm gonna have to get you a bucket, I think. This isn't the Hilton. There aren't bathrooms in every room."

He swung his arm to the left. "The head's over there. That's the communal bathroom for the crew. Got sinks and showers and toilets and stuff. But you guys need to stay out of sight. So . . . try not to eat or drink too much." He seemed to be enjoying this.

"I'll go get that bucket," he said. He disappeared down the corridor.

I shuddered. "How *kind* of him," I said. I looked at Hiro. "There's no *bathroom*. Or *sink*."

Hiro shrugged. "I don't know what else we can do. . . ."

"We're gonna be on this thing for how many days?" I sat on the bottom bunk. I knew that I'd been in worse situations than this, but the idea of being without a bathroom seemed just . . . *disgusting*.

"Maybe I'll be able to sneak to the head and change the water," Hiro suggested.

"Hmph," I said. I wondered if I would've been better off on my own, back in Tokyo. This whole thing was getting worse by the second. One false move and we were dead.

One tiny noise and they'd probably make us walk the plank.

Andy returned with a bucket and a small jug of water. "You'll have to make do with this," he said. Hiro grunted in thanks.

"What's that humming?" I said, pricking up my ears.

"You're right next to the torpedo room," Andy said blandly.

"The *what*?"

Andy crossed his arms, suddenly impatient. "I can't stand here and *explain* all of this to you," he said. "I've got to get out before all of us get killed. Just remember: Stay quiet, don't turn on any lights, and someone will come and get you in California when we've docked."

"What if there's an emergency? Like a collision or something? And people have to evacuate?" Hiro asked.

Andy looked at us and shrugged. "Tough shit," he said.

Then, without a good-bye, he left.

I flopped down on the bed. Above me Hiro tried to squeeze into his bunk.

"It'll be okay," he said. I could see, dimly, that he was really squashed in there, his legs bent at an unnatural angle. "I need to be more flexible anyway."

I rolled my eyes. "Such a martyr," I said. I was tense. This was creepy. We were next to a *torpedo room*? What if one of them detonated?

It was also super-cold in here. I wrapped my arms around myself and shivered. Andy had explained on the way down that the sub would be cold because it was powered by diesel fuel, but the fuel was much more critical for actually moving the sub toward its destination. Using the fuel for heat would be a waste.

Looking at my bunk—which was exactly the same size as Hiro's, just on the bottom—I started to panic. This ship should be renamed U.S.S. *Claustrophobia*. There were no windows, we'd be thousands of feet underwater, and although it was just a routine mission—going back to San Diego in order to switch crews—there could still be high seas danger.

They could find us. We were right next to the crew. All they had to do was come and unlock this door. . . .

I tried to lie down. The only way my legs would go straight was if I stuck them out the door. The pillow felt like a chunk of lead.

Titanic, this was not. *The Love Boat*, a definite no.

Later we heard all the crew members stomp on, clattering through their doors, bumping the walls, shouting at one another. I held my breath. They were walking right outside our door.

"No one is in this one?" a voice called. Then there was a knock on our door.

"Nope. Don't need it this time."

"Damn! Can I have my own room?"

I breathed in sharply.

"Very funny, McGuirk."

The two guys laughed and drifted away.

I settled back into my bed. The gloom of the situation

folded around me like a heavy fog. We would have to spend days in the muggy darkness, listening to people around us, with nothing to do. Fearing every moment that they might unlatch this door and find us.

The sub began to move. It was a subtle feeling, but it sounded like . . . more machines were whirring or something. The floor vibrated softly. I bit my lip. We were on our way. The crew quieted down, most likely going to man their various duties on the sub. Across the room I heard Hiro breathe out.

"I guess this is it," he whispered.

"There's no turning back now," I replied softly, and swallowed hard.

Pretty soon it really started to suck.

It felt like the sub was a cork bobbing on the rockiest seas known to man. Or like we were in a washing machine, going around and around and around, never stopping. I got so sick, I couldn't even see straight.

"I'm gonna throw up again," I said to Hiro, lunging toward the bucket. This was even more nightmarish than I'd thought it would be. Throwing up was bad enough when you had to do it in a toilet. But we only had a bucket and couldn't wash it away. The smell was making me even sicker.

"You have to try to stay quiet," Hiro said. Outside, we heard nothing. Some of the crew members were probably asleep. "They'll hear you throwing up."

"I don't care," I moaned. "Why didn't that ass Andy say anything about getting sick?"

Hiro stroked my hair after I pushed the bucket away. My body was covered in sweat; I felt it sticking to the back of my neck and to my arms. "I can't do this," I said. The room started to spin. My stomach began to lurch again.

Strange clicks and stomps boomed from the ceiling. I heard someone shout and gripped Hiro's hand.

And then a shrill, earsplitting alarm sounded. I perked up and almost screamed. The alarm was the loudest thing I'd ever heard. Were we being evacuated? Had something happened? I breathed in quickly.

But as soon as it had started, the alarm stopped. The air quieted again. I heard rustling in the room next to us.

"What was *that*?" I said.

"Maybe a wake-up call?" Hiro suggested.

"Oh *God*," I said. "You mean it could happen again?" At this point I didn't even care if the alarm was actually a siren telling everyone to evacuate or that we were being bombed. In this situation death would be much more comfortable than lying on the floor of the sub, sick as a dog.

My stomach lurched again. My sickness was starting to make me paranoid. "You're holding me prisoner here," I said to Hiro, bending over the bucket.

"No, I'm not," Hiro said.

"This is the worst torture ever," I said through my teeth. "Something about this just isn't right. Did Melissa poison me with this peanut butter?"

"You're just seasick," Hiro said. "It'll go away after a while. I promise."

"I should never have trusted you," I said wearily. "That military base . . . hiding under the bed . . . Melissa . . . God. This whole experience has been shady."

If I could just get off this sub, I rationalized, *I could go it alone.* I had the diamond necklace. I hadn't told Hiro about it. I just had to make it a couple more days.

But I felt so awful. "Ughhh . . . ," I groaned.

"You have to keep your voice down," Hiro said, stroking my hair again. "Just try and stay strong." One of the crew members was talking loudly to his bunkmate in the room next to us. I overheard the word *torpedo.*

"Don't touch my hair," I said nastily, flicking his hand away. "That's making me dizzy."

I started to cry. "I can't go on," I said. "I'm so tired of all of this. Everywhere I turn, it's more misery than the last place. At least as a prisoner of Masato's, I wasn't dizzy and puking every second. . . . Oh God . . ."

The sub lurched again. "Who the hell is driving this thing?" I wailed. "The yakuza?" I tried to laugh, but then I grew nervous. Was it possible?

"Of course not," Hiro said. "We have to be quiet."

I heard boots stomping around. A hissing sound of a valve opening seemed like it was right inside my ear. I saw mini-explosions in front of my eyes. My head hammered. I wondered if they were fiddling around in the torpedo room.

Hiro held me in his lap. I was too exhausted to move. "You're so beautiful," he said, looking down at me, the penlight making a tiny spotlight beside him.

"Are you crazy?" I said weakly. "This is *definitely* not the time for *that.*"

I must've looked frightful and smelled pretty wretched, too. Hiro didn't show any signs of sickness. And here he was, sitting on the grimy floor of a submarine with me, in the darkness, cleaning my throw-up from my face, dealing with the horrible smell of the room. I had to give him points for trying.

We sat in silence for about half an hour; then my nausea and paranoia subsided slightly. I tried to breathe evenly and deeply, willing away the sickness.

"So tell me about my mother," I said in a drowsy voice.

"I don't know anything at all about her," Hiro said. "All I know is that she lives in San Diego. But considering what a beautiful daughter she has, she must be gorgeous."

"Do you think we'll find her?" I asked, shrugging off his compliment.

"Yes, I do," he said. "We have to."

"How can you be so sure?"

"Because . . ." He paused. "This is a very important thing for you. We must try to find her. We must do everything it takes. We can't lose hope."

"Ughhh . . . ," I said, my stomach lurching again.

The sub rocked and then grew steady. For a moment my head felt clear. I sat up a little. Hiro looked at me and smiled. I grinned wearily back. In this half-light he looked vulnerable and small. His hands reached for my waist. He drew me gently to him.

"You really are the most beautiful person I've ever

seen," Hiro said. "I was devastated when I thought I'd lost you."

I laid my head on Hiro's neck, just as Melissa had. Which reminded me.

"Melissa really had it bad for you, huh?" I said.

"Well, maybe," he said, pausing. "We dated a couple of times. I broke it off with her, but we remained friends. But I think she wanted more."

"So you think she did you this favor because of her love for you?" I asked, my head still buried in his neck. He still smelled the same: woodsy, like incense, like someone who is in good shape and eats well.

"I don't know," he said modestly. "But she wasn't the girl for me."

He gave me a squeeze. My stomach stayed calm. I breathed out, not sure whether I should laugh or not. Hiro was serious. Hiro had been dead serious this whole time.

"I almost lost you," Hiro said again, sounding choked up. "But I escaped just in time."

Then I realized: Hiro was in the same predicament I was. He *had* to be, in some ways. Why would he have risked his life, running through that navy base, stowing away on a sub? It would be really stupid if he were risking all this just to kill me. Maybe I had to try and trust him.

I wiped off my mouth and looked up at him. Even though I was covered in puke and a downright mess, I grabbed the back of his neck and kissed him. I'm not sure what made me do it. It was a sad kiss. It wasn't the kisses we used to have—pure, clean, happy kisses. Kisses that said, "We've found each other!" No. This kiss was different. This kiss was confused and complicated and a little scared.

I backed up from Hiro. His eyes were surprised. He opened his mouth to speak but couldn't.

The sub shifted. We both jumped and were tossed in two different directions. I doubled over, clutching my stomach, and crawled onto the bunk. From far away I heard the sound of a warning alarm. And then quickly the sound of someone shutting it off.

Hiro shifted across the room. I looked for him in the darkness and found his shape. He was lying on his bunk bed. He clicked on the penlight and shone it over at me. His eyes bored into mine. The kiss was still hot on my lips. I could still taste him.

Then he quietly scrambled down from the bed, knelt down on the floor, and put his arms on my lap. He was trembling.

"I love you so much," he said. "I don't want anything bad to happen to you. Ever again."

"I love you, too," I said, although I had no idea if I meant it or not. I said it in fear that we would never survive this sub trip. In terror of what I'd been through and what might happen next.

Finally, after what seemed an eternity and a half, the tension growing thicker and thicker, both of us scared and charged and thinking the same thing, he leaned down and kissed me. I pulled him down to me. The world was quiet around us. Our mouths locked together, and for a brief moment I got a tiny glimpse of how I used to feel about Hiro. The same strong arms, the same earlobes, the same back of the neck. Here in the sub we were free and hidden and could do anything we wanted. No *banditos*, no ninjas, nothing. It was a luxury we'd never experienced before.

But I didn't know if I felt ready.

I didn't know if I loved him.

I didn't know if this was the right place. The right time.

Hiro kissed my face, my shoulders, my arms.

"What do you think . . . ?" he murmured, laying me back on the cold, gritty floor.

My heart pounded. What *did* I think? I felt confused, lost, afraid, screwed up. I remembered reading somewhere that people want to have sex when a loved one has died in order to prove that they are alive. I felt a little like that. I needed to prove I was alive, that I was strong, that I would get through this. I pawed Hiro, unsure of my actions, unclear about my feelings. I didn't love him. I did. I didn't trust him. And then I did trust him. Or did I? I couldn't decide.

Hiro kept kissing me. His kisses felt genuine and eager. I knew Hiro loved me with all his heart. I knew that he thought I was his ideal. But I had a feeling he was hiding something from me. I didn't know if he could protect me from this world or if he could even help me find my mother. My love for Hiro would never be the same as it had been before—clean, easy, pure. Now it had been marred by lies, the past, complications.

He managed to get my tank top off and began kissing my stomach and belly button. "Heaven," he called, crying.

Part of me felt dead inside. Part of me felt scared, sad, exhausted. Part of me still wanted him. And part of me hummed along, thinking of other stuff. *Do I have my birth mother's hair? Is Masato looking for me right now? Why does Mieko hate me so much? Are we going to get out of this alive?*

"Do you want this, too?" Hiro asked, still kissing me everywhere.

"I . . . ," I started. I wanted *something*. I needed something. I needed all this noise around me to stop. Just for a couple of minutes.

"Yeah," I answered finally.

Hiro sighed, ecstatic, and took me in his arms.

Later I lay awake, thinking. The sub groaned along. It was pitch-dark. With every little noise I jumped. A couple of guys were chattering away in the other bunk room. The little slice of light under the door shimmered red. Andy had explained that during the night, certain areas of the sub used only red lights to save energy.

Hiro snored beside me, his arm cradled around my head. We were both squashed into one bunk.

I sighed. Back in Japan, when I lived in my old house, sometimes I'd lie in bed, trying to figure stuff out. I'd stare at the ceiling, trying to make sense of everything. But my problems seemed so small and silly compared to the ones I had now. What had I worried about then? What mattered?

I felt empty and strange. So that was sex. That was it. I didn't regret it, but I just didn't *feel* anything. Ever since I'd realized I had feelings for Hiro, at least parts of me had desperately wanted to have sex with him. Now that we had, I felt detached from Hiro, as if I didn't know him anymore. But the truth was, I knew more about him than I ever had before. I knew his secrets, or at least some of them.

Yet I didn't feel that this was good enough.

I sat up and wriggled out of the bunk. My feet ground into the cold floor. I fumbled for the ladder and climbed into the top bunk, above where Hiro was sleeping. The springs squeaked. I shivered. Then I hung over the side of the bed and looked at Hiro. I could barely see him in the dim red light coming from the bottom of our doorway. But from what I could see, he seemed so peaceful lying there, his face calm and smooth, his hands curled like a baby's. But if I was going to be perfectly honest with myself, the same lust wasn't there anymore. There was an empty shell inside me. The shell was waiting something—someone?—else. I needed answers somehow.

I hoped I would find my mother. I hoped I would find something.

A fist of nerves seized in my chest. What in the world was I doing with my life?

And would my life ever be *normal*?

8

Fists pounded on our door. I shot up from the bed.

What day was it?

"Open up!" boomed a voice from the other side.

"What's happening?" I said quietly to Hiro. Had they found us?

It had to be days later. Neither of us wore a watch, but it felt like a lot of time had passed.

Hiro slipped down from his bunk and walked to the door. Through the dim light I saw him bend over. Only a few hours after we'd had sex, he'd gotten seasick and had suffered from it for what seemed like days. He'd had to use the same bucket I used. Neither of us had felt well enough to sneak out to the head to clean it up. I was surprised the crew next door didn't come knocking from the smell alone.

Slowly he slid the latch across and pushed open the door.

"Are you Hiro?" said a voice. I couldn't see anything. The

light was brighter out there than it was in here. I squinted, unused to it. My heart pounded. *They've found us,* I thought. *This could be it.*

"Yes," he said in a small, weak voice.

"I'm Dave. Andy contacted me."

I breathed out.

"Is everyone gone?" Hiro asked.

"Yeah," Dave said. I sat up straighter and could now see him. He was a tall guy with a buzz cut and long arms and legs. His face was stern. "We gotta go *now*, though. If we wait, the crew is gonna come back on and get her equipped to ship back."

"Okay," Hiro said.

Dave stepped back. "Didn't have your sea legs, huh?" he said, sniffing, making a disgusted face.

Hiro staggered into the hall. I climbed out of my bed. The hall lights, red and blinking, illuminated the corrugated-iron walkway. Dave strode quickly toward the hatch. I scurried to catch up.

"Is everything okay back at the base in Japan?" Hiro asked. "Everything all right with Andy? And Melissa?"

Dave didn't answer. He just kept walking.

We would have to go through the same process in reverse: rush through the sub, which was now illuminated in red, pass through the bright mess hall, climb up the slippery ladder to the top, splash into the water, avoid the guard's eye, and wade to shore. As I started to climb the ladder, my legs felt like jelly after a few days of disuse. I glanced over my shoulder and saw Hiro clutching his stomach.

At the top of the ladder I realized it was pitch-black out. The sub bobbed fitfully. The moon rose yellow and blurry over the harbor.

Dave had already splashed into the water.

Hiro, below me, touched my hand. "What's the matter?" he said.

"Nothing," I whispered. "It's just . . . so dark outside."

We crept off the ladder and onto the curved hull of the sub. I looked around. The guy who'd led us out, Dave, was gone. He'd already paddled the whole way in.

I looked down at the eerie black water. The waves lapped furiously. I couldn't tell how deep it was. I looked under the dock to see if the water was shallow, the way it had been in the Japanese sub dock. But it didn't seem so, and I didn't see anything to hold on to underneath the dock to help us to shore.

We'd either have to swim or take the dangerous way. The dock.

I glanced out at the shore. There was a little building there. A guy with a gun stood on guard. Another guy with a gun was smoking a cigarette. If we went over the dock, they'd see us.

My pulse started to race.

Hiro was looking down at the water, too. "How dangerous could it be?" he said.

"Swimming isn't exactly my strong suit," I said. "Remember my stunt in the ocean?"

"Yeah," Hiro said. Once when Hiro had challenged me to "accept my own death," I'd thought he meant "go out and try to kill yourself." I'd flung myself into the water when there was a riptide and nearly drowned.

I hadn't been in the water since. It freaked me out. I looked at it again. If we dawdled up here any longer, the guards might see us. With that, I lowered myself into the ocean.

The water was warm, much warmer than it had been in Japan. Immediately a wave knocked into me and I went under. I flailed my arms, grasping for something. I felt Hiro's hands pulling me up. I came to the surface, gasping for air.

"Hold on to me," Hiro said, paddling for the shore. We were under the dock. Another wave crashed over us. We went down again. I was terrified. I'd never been in the water at night. There could be sharks or something. We could die, and no one would know.

Accept your own death, I told myself, remembering what I'd been taught.

Soon we were able to touch bottom. The sand underneath me felt soft and slippery. I stood, but another wave knocked me over. I was soaked, weak, hungry, sick, and dirty. Hiro staggered ahead of me, feeling his back pocket, making sure the wave hadn't washed away his wallet. My bag was soaked through and through. Who knew what the stuff inside looked like by now?

We stayed low under the dock and were soon right beneath the guardhouse. We crept around the back side and ran up the embankment. I turned around. There was the sub, murky and strange, halfway out of the water. We'd made it. We'd arrived.

On the shore, safely away from the navy guards, my legs

collapsed under me. I sat down. "I feel like I haven't walked in years," I said. "I think my muscles have atrophied."

"I wish we could start training again," Hiro said, helping me up. "I realize this isn't the time to talk about it, but I feel that if we had been in better condition, we might have endured the sub trip better."

Training. A wave of dread washed over me. My eyes met his, and for a moment I flashed back to the sex and then back beyond that, to a time when I'd known nothing of Hiro's past. A simpler time, when we'd trained together. When he'd been my sensei.

But I didn't want Hiro to be my sensei again. Or did I? I was confused.

"This way," Hiro said. We were on another navy base and had to find our way out. Here were the same sorts of squat buildings, the same weird silence. But I could tell we were in America. The air around us just had that *feeling*. It was wonderful to be away from the stench of the sub.

Hiro and I rushed through the shadows until we came up to the gate and a tall cyclone fence.

"What do we do?" I whispered. "How do we get out?"

Hiro looked right and left. "Shinobi-iri, maybe," he said. He pointed out some shadows that we might be able to slip through undetected. The guard looked half asleep.

We crept toward the shadows and then did the ninja stealth walk, silently skulking, knees bent, not making any sudden movements. When the shadows faded, we dropped to the ground and dragged ourselves forward on our stomachs.

But then I heard the *click* of the safety of a gun.

I froze.

"Who's there?" said a voice. Gate guy. The gun was pointed right at us.

"We're not in his range of vision," Hiro whispered very softly.

"Show yourself or I'll shoot," he said.

"Let's creep around and get him from behind," Hiro said.

He was crazy. This guy had a *gun*. I followed Hiro, legs wet and shaking, until we were close enough to jump the guy. And in one movement Hiro grabbed him from behind and tossed the gun away.

I scurried to pick it up. The thing was heavy. I slung it over my shoulder.

The other guard lunged for us. "Who the hell are you?" he snarled, grabbing for his gun. I kicked it out of his hand before he could get to it.

Hiro had the other guy in a stronghold, paralyzing his arms. He planted his feet, ducked down, and flipped the guy backward so that he somersaulted in the air and landed with a bone-shattering thud. He groaned.

The guy I'd kicked came back, fists raised. But Hiro managed a kick to his jaw, knocking him down as well.

"Come on!" he said, grabbing my hand.

We were only a couple of yards away when we heard the shots.

"Shit," I said.

"Just keep running," Hiro said. "Stay in the shadows."

We ran in the darkness of trees, telephone poles, buildings.

Our footsteps rang out, quick and nervous. I couldn't control my breathing. The shots still came, fiery and blazing.

We rounded a corner and stopped. "I don't think they're coming," Hiro said, listening.

"Let's run farther," I said. So we did.

I didn't know how long we ran. For three miles, for six, for ten. I didn't know how we *could've* run so far since we'd eaten almost nothing in the days we were on the sub. Adrenaline pushed us along. Finally, in a seedy residential neighborhood far from the base, we stopped, wheezing, doubled over.

I edged into the glow from a streetlight, free. I coughed and suddenly felt dizzy. Tears sprang to my eyes. I brought my hands to my face and tried to control myself.

Hiro came up to me and gave me a huge hug. "It's okay," he said. "We made it. We're here."

His hug was passionate; he wanted more. I hugged him back wearily. I felt like this was rock bottom. The wind kicked up. Wet from the ocean, I shivered.

"Come on," Hiro said, patting my shoulder, then taking my hand. "Let's see if we can find somewhere to stay."

The El Penguino hotel was only a notch better than the sub berth. From the outside it looked like it had been built in the 1800s and never renovated. A neon sign flickered Vacancy. A large woman in a flower-print muumuu manned the desk.

But it was all we could afford with the limited amount of money we had. The lady at the front desk eyed us suspiciously, as if she knew who we were and that we'd illegally entered the country on a submarine. Then slowly she handed us the key. We turned away and quickly walked to our room.

"Why was she looking at us as if we're criminals?" I said.

"Probably everybody who stays here is a criminal," Hiro said. He kept looking right and left nervously.

"Do you think someone's following us?" I asked.

Hiro shrugged.

We swung open the door. The knob was falling off. And there was a giant cockroach in the tub. When I saw it, I screamed. Then I smashed it with my shoe.

At least there *was* a bathroom.

I peeled my clothes off down to my underwear and filled up the sink with water and laundry soap from a little El Penguino complimentary toiletries kit. There was only one flake of soap, but I didn't care. I threw all my clothes in the sink to soak. The motel wasn't the type of place that offered bathrobes, so I wrapped myself in a dingy towel and flopped down on the bed.

I could hear the neon Vacancy sign buzzing out the window.

"I guess we'll stay here until we figure something else out," Hiro said. "Maybe until we find your mom."

I sighed. Finding my mother had seemed like an optimistic idea when we'd been in Japan. Now that we were here, having gone through what we'd just gone through, it seemed impossible. Who would help us track her down? I racked my brain to think of people I knew in San Diego. There *was* Detective Wachter. My mind flicked back to the last time I'd seen him. When I'd set up Teddy.

"Hey," I said to Hiro, who was counting his remaining money. "Was Teddy in Japan?"

He looked over at me, surprised. "Not that I know of," he said.

"Your father didn't mention anything?"

"I thought he was dead."

I'd neglected to tell Hiro about my adventure with Teddy right before Masato had brought me back to Japan. I'd been set up to frame Teddy and collect information that he'd been part of a major drug deal, but I'd told him to run instead.

"So he's *not* dead?" Hiro asked.

I opened my mouth to explain all this but then groaned. There was too much to tell. "Come on," I said. "If you're as connected as you seem to be, you must know for a fact that Teddy's not dead."

"I thought we went through this," Hiro said, frustrated. "I'm *not* all that connected."

I drew in my breath. Ouch. I'd hit a nerve.

"*Sorry,*" I said, pulling the towel around me.

"I guess I did know," Hiro said after a minute. He put his wallet down. "I just didn't know . . . that you knew."

"Hiro . . . ," I said weakly. "Why do you *keep* things from me? Like . . . why did you hide all that stuff from me about you? Why didn't you tell me anything about your family's ties to the yakuza when we were in L.A.? I mean, it seemed like you told *Melissa* about that . . . and you didn't tell me . . . I don't know . . . any of it. . . . Don't you realize that makes me trust you *less*? That it hurts my *feelings*?"

Hiro sighed, still tense. "I don't know. I'm sorry. I didn't tell you things because they're complicated. I didn't want to scare you off right away. I didn't mean for things to turn out . . . the way they did." He didn't seem to want to talk about this.

"But I *didn't* tell Melissa anything," he continued. "She's a bullshitter. She pretends like she knows everything about everyone even if she only has half a clue. It's not like I went around bragging about my past and where I came from." His face reddened. "Why do you think I *came* to this country? Why do you think I studied to become a samurai?"

"Okay, okay, *sorry*," I said. "You're right."

Hiro didn't answer. He paced angrily back and forth.

And then after a while he said: "But there are other things I need to tell you. Things I couldn't talk about on the sub. I thought the crew might've heard too much talking."

Silence. I rolled over, not facing him.

"There's something big," he said.

"What is it?" I asked, tensing up.

"I came back to Japan in order to find you, but I had to go through my father. He gave me the money to go there, and I knew he'd give me some inside information on what was going on with Masato and Mieko. But when I met him . . . he assumed that I would join the business. And with joining the business came initiation . . . if you know what I mean."

"Don't tell me you got initiated," I said, sitting up. "If you did, I'll never speak to you again. I'm outta here."

"No, no, I didn't. It was set for the night after I came for you. That's what Aki was talking about in Kabukicho, remember?"

."Oh . . . ," I said. "Yes, that's right. I wanted to ask you about that."

"I escaped just in time," Hiro said. "Luckily. I don't know what would've happened if . . ."

He trailed off and pulled his T-shirt over his head. His washboard stomach was still a little wet from sweat and the ocean.

I wondered if somewhere deep down, Hiro secretly *wanted* to get initiated. I looked at him and shuddered. Our intimacy on the boat—Hiro taking my shirt off, Hiro kissing my stomach—flashed through my head. I quickly shoved it away, a little disgusted.

"So what *else* did you find out about Masato and Mieko?" I asked. "Anything you haven't told me?"

"Well, the consensus is that Mieko has never liked you," Hiro said.

"I could've told you that one," I said, mustering a laugh. "She treats me like she's a lion and I'm a zebra. She wants to gnaw on my leg, I think."

"Also, according to my father, Mieko is heading up Konishi's company."

"She's heading up Kogo Industries," I repeated.

"You didn't know that?"

I rolled my head around. "Maybe. I don't know. I mean . . . it makes sense. She was all dressed up when I saw her. Businesswomanlike."

"And you might not want to hear this, but she's telling the press that you're dead."

"I'm dead?" I said. "That's a good one. I just saw her

a couple of days ago. How does she explain that?"

"She denies it, of course. She says she didn't see you. At first she told the press that yes, you were alive and things were happy. But now she's telling the press that the reports she got were wrong and that you *aren't* alive. You're dead. My father says it's to swing the stock price of Kogo, Inc., and that I could get in on the deal if I wanted to. Those who know when the price is going to change make a ton of money. I refused, of course."

"Wait, I don't get it," I said. "They're using *me* being alive or dead to affect the stock price?"

"She tells the press you're alive, business is good, the CEO is happy, the stock goes up. She tells the press there are now rumors that you're dead, which means the CEO is upset and business is bad, and the stock goes down. The yakuza investors make a killing because they know what she's gonna say before the public does."

"That's disgusting," I said. I didn't know what was worse: Mieko manipulating the stock market or Mieko claiming I was dead. She'd done something similarly weird before. She'd taken me shopping to Isetan, a rare event. I'd headed straight for the junior apparel section, trying on anything I could get my hands on. I'd been right in the middle of trying on an awesome Free People shirt when all of a sudden a voice came crackling over the loudspeaker.

"Heaven Kogo, please report to the information booth. Mieko is looking for you."

I'd thought it a little strange then. Why hadn't she said, *Your mother is looking for you?* Didn't those messages usually just say *your mother*? No, she'd said *Mieko*, as if she was a com-pletely cold person, isolated from me. It was weird.

And to add to the weirdness, when I'd turned up at the information booth, after getting a stern look from Mieko, the woman at the booth had smiled and said, "Oh, how cute. You two look so much alike. Is this your daughter?"

And Mieko had looked at her and said, very sharply, "No."

Yikes, I thought now. She had a heart of ice.

"So your father wanted you to get in on it?" I asked.

"Yes," Hiro said. "But I promise you, I didn't."

I paused. This was heavy stuff.

He continued to talk. "She also hates Konishi. I mean, I guess you realize that by now. Otherwise she . . . they . . . wouldn't be . . ."

I nodded, understanding. A twinge of terror and regret ran through me. I'd forgotten about my father in the last cou-ple of days. Would anyone be able to stop them from . . . doing whatever they were doing? Were they *really* killing him?

The strange thing was, I'd never noticed Mieko doing anything mean to my father. I couldn't quite believe she was trying to *kill* him. They weren't exactly the most *together* couple . . . they never were affectionate in public, and Mieko often went on extensive spa leaves at a moment's notice, basically staying way out of the picture . . . but they had to have *some* love for each other. Right?

"Do you think Masato really has anything to do with this?" I said.

"Yes, I do."

"I don't know." I thought this out. "Masato wouldn't shut up about how he just wanted me to 'relax' the whole time. Maybe that's what Mieko told him this was all about . . . relaxing. Maybe she said, 'Take her to your house since her old home is far too stressful right now, with her father sick.'"

I could feel Hiro's hands tighten up. "I don't exactly think that's it," he said.

"Yeah? You think Masato was more in on things?"

"I . . . I do."

"How do you know?"

Hiro was silent.

"I just do," he said. "I . . . I can't explain. Not yet."

He sounded on the verge of tears.

"Well, all right," I said. "Maybe he does know something. I mean, there was some guy in Roppongi the other day who clearly looked yakuza who had a gun pointed at my head. And I'm betting Masato had a hand in that. He was the one, after all, who conned Kaori into taking me to Roppongi in the first place. Of that I'm sure."

Hiro remained silent.

"It scares me to think what they're doing to my father," I said.

I thought of something else. "Oh my God," I said, clapping a hand over my mouth. "Do you think . . . do you think they both had something to do with Ohiko?"

Hiro lowered his eyes. "It's very possible," he said.

"It makes sense," I said, my voice choked. "They want the business, right? They've probably always wanted it! And Ohiko was next in line after my father. . . ."

"So they had to make sure he was out of the picture," Hiro said ruefully.

"Oh God," I said. "This is all about my father's stupid *business!*"

"It's ironic, too, since Ohiko didn't even *want* to work for your father."

"They probably thought he'd change his mind. And there were so many others they could pin this on, you know? Yakuza, angry that he wouldn't join; the Yukemuras . . . other families . . . enemies of my father . . ."

I balled my fists. "I hate them," I said. "It's all about greed and money. That's all that matters to them. Masato and his sports cars and Mieko and her . . . and her new *clothes.* It's sickening."

We sat there in silence for a long time. The neon continued to buzz. A couple in the room next to us started yelling at each other. In the room to the other side someone was watching a boxing match at maximum volume.

"I miss my brother," I said, a little out of nowhere. "I loved him so much."

"I know," Hiro answered. "He loved you, too."

We sat on the bed. I could feel Hiro moving a little closer to me. I could tell what he wanted. But I couldn't respond. I knew I'd just have to *reach over* and kiss him, and it would all start again.

But I didn't want that.

So instead I flopped down on the pillow. "I'm exhausted," I said. "I want to go to sleep."

"There's only one bed . . . ," Hiro said flirtatiously, flopping down beside me.

"You can sleep next to me—I don't mind," I said. And then I snuggled under the covers and closed my eyes. I *was* exhausted. I hadn't slept well on the sub. To be in a real bed, on something that wasn't moving, was a wonderful feeling.

I felt Hiro beside me, frustrated. But I kept my eyes closed. He stroked my hair. I could tell he was looking at me. I could tell he was dying to kiss me, to be closer to me. But instead he burrowed under the covers with me and snapped the light off.

Even though my body was tired, my mind was still reeling from all the news I'd just heard—about Hiro's almost initiation, Masato, Mieko's bloodlust for my father, Ohiko's killers revealed. It was all freaking me out.

Talking about all this had also revived the memory of Ohiko again. I could almost see him standing beside us, as plain as day. His hair was the same as it had been when he died, somewhat long, hanging in his face. He was wearing his traditional white gi, as if he'd come fresh from the dojo.

I so badly wanted to ask him things. *Can you help me with any of this?*

Did you know about Hiro? Should I trust him?

And the big one. *Was it Mieko who had you killed?*

But Ohiko stayed silent. I blinked, and he wasn't there anymore. I was getting no answers. I wondered if anything would ever be resolved in this big, terrible mystery. Or would I just have to keep running?

What would happen when there was nowhere left to run?

I started to grow sleepier. The pillow was surprisingly

soft. The buzzing of the neon seemed quieter now, less obtrusive. The couple next door had stopped fighting.

"There's one more thing I need to tell you," Hiro said, his voice wiry and thin.

"Huh?" I said. Now I was dead tired. Hiro's voice sounded like it was in a tunnel, far, far away.

"I . . . ," Hiro started. But then his voice moved even farther away. I drifted into a fitful, deep-sea sleep. Whatever he said next, if he said anything at all, I didn't hear.

I woke up around six and lay in bed, next to Hiro, staring at the ceiling. I could hear the sounds of the highway out the window. I wondered where we were in San Diego. I wondered if Detective Wachter was still on the job and if he was, would he help me out?

Hiro finally woke up. He propped himself on his elbow and smiled at me, the coy way the boys do in movies the morning after they've slept next to the girl of their dreams. I felt acutely like I was *in* a scene at that moment—that this moment had nothing really to do with me.

"Hey," he said.

"Hi," I said.

He kissed me. I blinked. I felt nearly ready to cry. I should have been feeling something delicious and wonderful, but I felt hollow and cold. He grabbed for me, but I backed away.

"How about some morning stretches?" I asked.

He sat up. "Okay," he said slowly.

Hiro led a peaceful set of tai-chi-type movements. It was nice, actually. Quite therapeutic to slowly circle my hands in the grasp-sparrow's-tail and push-and-press-forward moves. Hiro was *still* a good teacher.

When we finished, I sat back down on the bed, eager to do some more training. My body felt rickety and sluggish, but the stretches had really reawakened my desire. I wanted to kick and jab and move.

"So," I said. "I guess I *am* still interested in training."

"That's good," Hiro said, his eyes sparkling. "So you still want a sensei, eh?"

"Maybe," I said, although I wasn't sure if I wanted it to be Hiro. "Do you have the next mission for me?"

"Mission?" he asked, surprised.

"Yeah. You know . . . be invisible, accept death, harness your brainpower. That stuff."

"I don't have any other missions for you," Hiro said quietly.

"What?" I said.

He sat down next to me. "You've learned everything you can from me. In my opinion, your journey is nearly complete. Now you know your enemy."

"I *do*?" I said. And then I realized—I did.

"Huh," I said.

"You're free," Hiro said. "In fact, I should be learning from *you*." He looked at me with such desire. I bit my lip. Hiro had just told me, flat out, that I was better than he was. I wondered if in many ways I had been attracted to Hiro because he was my teacher, because he was wiser than I was. But now . . . who was Hiro? Who was he in relation to me? Was I now better than he was? End of story? Was that enough for me?

It wasn't.

Hiro bent down and reached for the edge of my T-shirt, wrapping his arms around my waist. He drew me closer into him. I could still smell the ocean in his hair.

He started kissing my neck. It felt strange and slippery. His hands slid up under my T-shirt. His legs gripped me closer to him.

I pushed him away.

Hiro looked up. "What's the matter? Don't you want . . . ?"

I couldn't answer. How could I explain this?

"I . . . ," I started. Then I lowered my eyes and shook my head.

Hiro searched for a clue in my face, and then suddenly he realized. "I see," he said. "Oh." His voice sounded choked.

I wished there were words to express how I was feeling, but I was so confused. We looked at each other for a while, not speaking. Finally my eyes dropped to the ground. I couldn't get the spark back. As hard as I tried, as much as I wanted to, I couldn't.

"I just don't know," I mumbled.

"I don't understand," Hiro said. "Why did you want to . . . on the sub?"

"I'm not sure, okay?" I said, frustrated. "Maybe it was a mistake."

"Oh," Hiro said sharply. "A mistake. I see. I'm just a mistake to you."

"No . . . ," I said, still not looking at him. "That's not what I mean. But . . . I don't know if I want to do this."

"Well, what *do* you want?"

That was a good question.

"All I know is that I don't want this," I said, my voice low and dead.

Hiro sighed loudly and turned away.

I flopped back on the bed and stared at the ceiling. I heard Hiro rustling around in his bag. Finally he turned back to me. I was shocked to see that his face looked red and glossy—as if he'd been crying.

"There are many things I've given up for you," he said. He almost sounded angry.

"Look, I'm *sorry*. . . ."

"You don't even realize," he said. His tone of voice turned from anger to hopelessness. "The things I've done. . . . Heaven, it's not all good. I'm not all good."

"Come on," I said, sitting up. "That's ridiculous. You've gotten away from that. That's why you've come here. You told me so last night! Even if we can't be together in the way you want, you've still escaped from . . . from *that* over there in Japan. Right? I mean, even if we can't be . . . you know . . . like *that* with each other, it still doesn't mean this has all been for nothing."

Hiro sighed loudly. We didn't speak again for a while.

"I still want to help you," he said softly. "I want to help you find your mother."

"Thanks," I said, although I wasn't sure if I wanted his help.

Hiro groaned, sensing my hesitation. "I'm going out for a little while," he said.

And before I could say anything, he slammed the door.

I lay back on my pillow and bit the edge of my hand. Then I stared out the window at the happy, warm San Diego sun and tried to think of nothing. I stared at it for so long that I started to get big, blinding spots in front of my eyes.

9

I decided to call Detective Wachter for help with my mother. He'd been willing to assist me when I was in jail. It was worth a shot to ask him for support in this crazy situation. I looked up the number for the San Diego police station in the phone book and punched in the digits.

"Heaven Kogo," he said when he picked up the phone. "I had a feeling you'd be back. That uncle of yours couldn't hold you for long, huh?"

I prayed he wouldn't ask any questions, and he didn't. I explained about my mother. "Do you think there's any way that I could track her down?"

"Hmmm," Wachter said. "Do you know who your father is?"

"Well, no," I said. "Not my birth father."

There was a long pause. Finally he spoke again. "I know someone at UC San Diego who's working on something like this. He uses his research more for antiterrorism reasons, but he does a lot of stuff with the police and could probably run a couple of tests on you. Let me call him and see when he's available."

"Great," I said, wondering what these "tests" would be.

We arranged that he would pick me up in his car about three hours later. Hiro reappeared in the hotel room, avoiding my eyes, still looking miserable. I wondered how in the world we were going to stay in the same room together after this. I told him about Detective Wachter and that I'd be starting the investigation.

Immediately he said, "I want to go with you."

"No, really, you don't have to," I argued. I wanted to do this by myself.

"No . . . I want to," Hiro said. He looked up at me imploringly. "Please."

"Fine," I growled, annoyed. I didn't know why I was so upset with Hiro. After all, without him, I wouldn't even have been in San Diego on this great search for my mother. Still, I found myself wanting to leave him behind. I was scared that if I trusted him for too long, he'd only end up disappointing me.

I waited at the curb. Hiro and I stood together but with a space between us. Detective Wachter pulled up and honked his horn. I ran to get in the front seat. Hiro slumped in the back.

"You're looking a little thin," he said.

"I was at a spa for a week," I told him. "Strict diet. Then I got seasick. Don't ask."

I gave him a once-over. Tall, square jaw, sorta Dick Tracy–like. He wore a Lacoste shirt and Dockers pants. Sort of a mix between a cop and a soccer dad.

"You look exactly the same," I told him. Hiro sat in the back, silent. He was still feeling awkward about our conversation in the hotel room.

We drove to a squat-looking lab building of the UCSD campus. Inside, I sniffed. "It smells like school," I said. "It's funny—whatever country you're in, school smells the same."

While Detective Wachter pressed on ahead of me, Hiro didn't leave my side. We passed a lot of identical-looking classrooms: each of them had a blackboard, a desk, tables, and lab equipment. I peeked into one room and saw various animals in cages. In another there was a guy with electrodes on his head, walking on a treadmill.

"Lots of testing done here," Wachter said.

I shot a look at Hiro. I could tell he was still hurt and annoyed. One part of me wanted to take his hand and reassure him that things would be fine. But another part of me didn't.

We came to a doorway; through it I could see a slew of cameras, computers, printouts, papers, and giant screens. A man sitting at one of the computers with some weird goggles on his eyes didn't look up as we came in. Finally Wachter cleared his throat. The guy ripped the goggles off his face, causing some of his hair to stand up haphazardly from his skull. He smiled crookedly at us. One eye was slightly bigger than the other. He looked like he could have stepped off the set of *The X Files*.

"Heaven, Hiro, this is Professor Clarkson," Wachter said.

The professor stuck out his hand. He studied my face very carefully. "Interesting," he said.

"What?"

"Nothing," he replied, shaking his head quickly. He looked at me again, his eyes widening. "You have an interesting face, that's all."

I felt like a lab rat. Hiro gave me a small smile for support.

"She's searching for her birth mother," Wachter explained. "There is evidence that her mother is in San Diego and gave birth in the area. Is that right, Heaven?"

"I think," I said.

"Okay, this is what we're going to do," Clarkson said, bustling around, moving papers from one table to another. He finally found what he was looking for: a wand-shaped camera.

"There is a technique that has been used for quite some time now, called biometrics. It's a method of scanning parts of the body in order to 'identify' you. You might remember the facial recognition systems used at the Super Bowl in 2001?"

I shrugged, not knowing too much about football. And 2001 seemed about twenty million years ago.

"That's right," Hiro said. "Video cameras were scanning and analyzing every face that went through the gates to go to the game."

"Yes," Clarkson said. "Instantly those hundreds of thousands of people who went through the gates were put into the facial recognition system. This is how it works: Your face is scanned into a digital camera and the distances between certain parts of your face, like your eyes, nose, and mouth, are computed. If there is a face already stored in the system that matches, the computer calls it up."

I nodded. This sounded like something from *Star Trek* or *Terminator*.

"So that's the first thing we'll do," Clarkson said. "It's possible that your mother is not in our system, and this technology isn't perfect yet, so we might find matches that aren't her. But we have done a lot of secret scanning in the San Diego area—in banks, in sports arenas, et cetera—so many people are in our database."

"Cool," I said.

"Professor Clarkson works with the police quite often," Wachter said behind me. "This device has really been put into place to prevent terrorism, and it's helped us catch a fair number of criminals."

"Hopefully my mother's not a criminal," I said, making a joke. No one laughed.

Clarkson had me stand about two feet in front of some type of digitized instrument. He stared into it for a long time. I heard a lot of weird beeps coming from it.

"What's it doing?" I asked.

"Try to stay still," he said. "It's measuring you."

Next Clarkson asked for a small sample of my hair. "We can use this to match your DNA with that of people in the area. At the moment, certain hospitals have DNA records of all the patients who have passed in and out of them over the last ten years." He held up a tiny piece of metal. "See this?" he asked.

"Not really," I said, squinting.

"This is the size of the chip that can analyze your DNA versus our catalog of DNA in seconds."

"Whoa," I said. I wasn't a particularly sciencey kind of girl, and I wasn't a big science-fiction reader. This stuff seemed absolutely over the top.

Clarkson also instructed me to put my handprint on an electronic pad and speak clearly into a digital recording device. "Banks are beginning to use voice-recognized PIN numbers," he explained. "We have a log of different voices that match up to different people in the system. There's a chance that the different intonations of your voice will match your mother's—that happens often. One sister gets access to the other sister's accounts. Mothers to daughters', too."

"That doesn't seem very safe," I said.

"Well, as I say, the technology isn't perfect yet," Clarkson said. "But we will have a very good chance with all of these different tests to narrow down your choices to maybe a hundred or so."

"A hundred?" I said. I'd have to go through a hundred people?

"But then we can narrow the results down further," Wachter interrupted. "We can get hospital records of who gave birth in San Diego less than twenty years ago. If those records match any of the names on our list, you could be down to only a few choices."

"It's a good thing I'm a little under twenty," I said. "My birthday's in about a week."

"That might help us, too," Clarkson said. "We might be able to pinpoint at what date the people on the list gave birth."

"Although," Hiro said, "who knows if your birthday is *really* your birthday, right?"

"That's true," I said. My father had always said April 8 was my birthday, but what if he'd been making things up?

Which led me to think briefly of something else. I was here looking for my birth mother. But who was my birth *father?*

I saw out of the corner of my eye that Hiro was gazing at me with lust and hurt. I shot my eyes away. How could he love me if he didn't have any idea who I was?

I sat in a chair while Dr. Clarkson fiddled with his computer, pulling up records, making matches. His brow furrowed as he squinted at the screen. I heard my voice from the recognition sample echo again and again. He tried it against several women's voices. None of them sounded like mine.

Finally he pulled out a list of about twenty-five names. "I was able to access the hospital records database online, and so I did the match," he said.

I looked at the list. None of the names jumped out at me.

"Basically what you're looking at is a list of women who gave birth nearly twenty years ago in the San Diego area and who have either been in the hospital since, had their face scanned by a video camera, or used voice-activated PIN numbers." He shuffled around a bit.

"I can't guarantee that any of these people is your birth mother," he said. "And I can't guarantee that any of these people even still *live* in the San Diego area. But this is the best technology we've got at present."

"Thanks," I said.

"Yes, thank you," Hiro said.

I left, feeling a little nonplussed. "It's creepy to think that we're being watched and scanned and monitored at every second of the day," I said. It was like Masato's house—all those video cameras.

Wachter studied the list. "I can run this through our address finder back at the station. We'll find out where these women live and get their phone numbers. It'll take about five minutes."

Back in front of the station, Hiro froze in his tracks. I followed his gaze. There was a guy across the street, talking on his cell phone, staring at us.

"Who is that?" I asked. He looked familiar.

"I don't know," Hiro said. He scuttled inside.

I peered out at the guy. Where did I know him from? He was really *glaring* at Hiro. Was he someone from the dojo or something?

I sat down on a chair in the station as Detective Wachter went into his office to pull up some files. Another detective came through the front door, and a whoosh of warm air streamed in from the outside. I glanced at the cell phone guy. Still there. And in the split second the door was open, I heard him say something very loudly.

"Listen, Kaori. . . ."

"Kaori?" I whispered. I looked out again. The guy was gone.

"What did you say?" Hiro asked. He rubbed his hands together quickly.

"Nothing . . . ," I said, trailing off. There could be thousands of Kaoris. I looked out the window again. Maybe I didn't know that guy. I couldn't place him. My haragei wasn't indicating that he was super-dangerous.

It was probably just a coincidence.

Hiro jiggled his leg and up down. "Relax," I said, annoyed. "What are you so keyed up about?"

"I'm just uneasy, that's all," Hiro said. "Something doesn't feel right."

Wachter called me into his office, telling Hiro to stay outside. I shrugged at him and walked in alone.

He shut the door. "Here's the list," he said. "It's narrowed down to about fifteen people. I don't know what happened to the others; I was only able to get about four additional addresses. I can give you the addresses for the other six people, too, if you want, although it looks like three of them have relocated across the country and the other three live at least eight hours away."

"Thanks," I said, taking the list, barely looking at it.

"I want to talk to you about something else, though," he said. "Teddy."

"Teddy?"

"Yes." He looked at me suspiciously. I shivered for a moment, then stared him down. Wachter didn't know that I'd let Teddy go willingly. He thought that Teddy had threatened me, been wise to the action some other way, and brushed me off.

"Have you seen him?" he asked.

"No," I said. "I mean, I've wondered where he could

have gone, but I've heard nothing. I even asked Hiro about him, but . . ."

"Well, as you remember, he knew somehow that we were on to him," Wachter said. "He's split the L.A. area, probably a smart move. He's managed to evade us for quite some time. But look, if he gets wind that you're back, there's a chance he might want to come and talk to you, right? After all, you were almost married."

"Maybe . . . ," I said. My heart started to pound, and I felt a lump in my throat.

"Don't worry," Wachter said, noting my nervousness. "I won't put you through that again if I don't have to. But if you *do* see him, you're required to talk to me about it. You know that, right? I'm the one who supported your visa here in the States. I'm the one who pushed the papers through. And I'm the one who's helping you now. So you owe me. Do we understand each other?"

"Sure," I said, my voice quivering a little. I pushed back my fears and worries. I'd deal with Teddy when the time came. *If* the time came. If Teddy knew what was good for him, he'd be far, far away from here.

But a spark of curiosity glimmered in my head. I wondered where he might be.

"I've got some time this afternoon," Wachter said, leading me out of his office. Hiro stood quickly.

"I can drive you kids around to some of these addresses," Wachter added.

"That would be great!" I said. I looked at the paper for the first time. I didn't know San Diego at all and wasn't really sure where any of these houses might be. Were they houses in swanky neighborhoods or houses in the ghetto? What did my mom *do* for a living?

I noticed as we drove through the South Bay section of San Diego that Hiro kept looking out the car window nervously. "What is your *problem*?" I said.

"Nothing," he said quickly.

"First house is on Seacoast Drive," I said. "The name is Matthews. Melinda Matthews. Do you know where that is?"

"Sure," Wachter said. "It's not a far drive from here."

"Melinda Matthews," Hiro said. "Sounds like she could be a newscaster. Or a model."

"Doesn't sound like a Melinda Matthews would give birth to a Heaven Kogo," I said doubtfully.

"You never know," Wachter said.

When we came to the house, my face twisted up in confusion. The place was a dump. The front steps were crumbling, the paint job was messy, the yard was completely unkempt. Kids' toys—strollers, bikes, squeezy things, a kiddie pool, a swing set—littered the grass. "Yikes," I said. If this was my mother's house, then I might have half brothers and sisters.

I looked at Wachter and Hiro. "What should I do?" I said.

"Go ring the doorbell," Hiro urged.

I got out of the car and walked up the front path. I heard kiddie screams from inside.

Okay, focus. I realized my hands were shaking. What in the world should I say?

I stood there for a few moments. I felt Hiro and Wachter staring at me. Finally I rang the doorbell.

No one came.

I rang it again. Twice.

At last the door opened. I looked down. It was a little girl in pink overalls and messy pigtails. She had something—pudding?—all over her face.

"Hello," she said.

"Hi," I said. "Um . . ." My heart still pounded. *What do I do now?*

A frazzled woman with bleached blond hair and a World's Greatest Mom T-shirt peeked around the corner from the kitchen. I guessed this was Melinda Matthews, world-famous news anchorwoman. "Sadie, get back here," she said. "Stop opening the door to strangers."

Sadie ran back into the kitchen. I stood there like a dumbass.

"What do you want?" she asked. A baby screamed from inside.

"I—I . . . ," I stammered. I was completely tongue-tied.

"We're not interested in whatever you're selling," she said.

"Uh . . ." There was no way Melinda could be my mother. From the looks of it, she had about ten kids. Why would she give up an extra one?

"Wrong house," I finally blurted, and shut the door.

I walked back to the car, my hands up in hopelessness. "Something about that just didn't seem right," I said.

"She looked nothing like you," Hiro said. "We could see her from back here."

"Yeah," I said.

Hiro looked out the back window, agitated. "There's that blue car again," he said.

"What blue car?" Wachter asked. "You're sure cagey for such a kid. You on drugs or something?"

"Hiro, drugs?" I said, laughing. "Doubtful."

"Is it that cell phone guy from the station?" I whispered.

"No . . . I think it's two guys," Hiro said. Then he looked at me, brow furrowed. "Did you know who that cell phone guy was?"

"No," I said. "Did *you*?"

"No . . . ," he said, trailing off. But it sounded like he did.

"The next house, oddly enough, is only a couple of blocks from here," Wachter said. "You up for it?"

"What the hell," I said. "Let's go. But this time you come with me, Hiro. I got tongue-tied back there."

"Deal," Hiro said.

But the next house—apartment complex, to be exact—didn't look promising, either. I had to buzz apartment 4B—Jennifer Cage—from an intercom. I buzzed and buzzed and buzzed. Finally someone answered.

"What?" came a craggy voice.

Great. What should I say now? I looked at Hiro.

"Say you're Heaven Kogo," he whispered.

"It's Heaven Kogo," I said. Would this ring a bell?

"Who?" the person said.

I frowned at Hiro. "Heaven *Kogo*," I said louder, stressing my last name.

"I don't know a Heaven Kogo," the woman said. "Who are you?"

"Should we leave?" I whispered to Hiro. "This is a little ridiculous."

"Yeah," Hiro said.

We walked down the path back to the car. The day was perfect—sunny, not humid. The sun dappled through the trees; everything looked clean and fresh. San Diego seemed like a far more chill city than L.A. I hoped my mother would turn up somewhere. This was really a place I could get used to. It was so . . . so peaceful. And quiet.

Wait. Too quiet.

Suddenly I heard a twig snap.

Then a figure dropped from the sky.

Then another. Then another.

Six men, cloaked in black, the same as they always were. Fear clutched my throat.

It all happened in absolute slow motion. I looked at Hiro. He raised his eyebrows. All the blood had run from his face. I opened my mouth but couldn't speak.

I backed away, expecting them to follow me. But they didn't.

Instead they turned and surrounded Hiro. He looked scared, but he almost looked like he had been expecting this.

"Wha . . . ?" I croaked.

"Uyemoto," one of them growled. "You did not fulfill your duty." He held up a long bunch of pale blond curly hair. "So we found your little friend in the navy."

I gasped. Melissa.

"Now we've come for you," another ninja said.

I stayed back, surveying the scene. No one had raised a

finger yet. They all circled Hiro like wild animals on the Serengeti.

"And Miss Heaven Kogo." Another turned to me. He wore a purple sash around his waist and seemed to be more whittled and fit than the others. I backed away.

"Hiro had a duty to do. Did you know that?" he snarled. "And he *failed*."

Hiro lurched into the one who was talking. He kicked him right in his throat; purple sash was caught completely off guard. He staggered backward, grabbing his neck, bumping into the wall.

But five other people pounced on Hiro pronto. I came behind one of them and grabbed him around the waist. I planted my feet and threw him behind me.

Purple sash had recovered and barreled into Hiro. They began fighting fiercely. Hiro's face was intense and worried. I managed to fend off some others and drag them away from Hiro. But really, they had no interest in me. They all hungrily swarmed back to Hiro, as if they were trained robots or something.

Hiro didn't seem to be fighting very hard. He wasn't blocking simple moves. I cringed as I saw blood fly from his nose.

What the hell was happening?

"Freeze!" came a scream from behind me. I turned around. Wachter. He cocked the trigger of his gun. Immediately one of the ninjas tackled him. They rolled for a while. The gun flew off into the bushes and fired. I ducked, hoping not to get hit with a stray bullet. But when I looked up, it looked like the bullet hadn't hit anyone.

Hiro continued to battle the purple-sashed guy. The others just stood around, watching. Purple sash was really giving it to him, dirty street fighting, pounding his knuckles— which, I noticed, had a lot of rings on them—into Hiro's face.

This was ridiculous. I had to do something. I ran into purple sash and climbed on his back, battering him from behind. But he was powerful. He shook me off effortlessly. I landed back on the ground with a thump. My hip screamed out in pain.

As I sat there, groaning, another ninja stepped over me and started giggling. "What's so *funny*?" I cried.

"You're trying to defend him," the ninja said in a slick, silvery voice. "You stupid, silly girl. Don't you know that he was sent to set you up?"

"To kill you," another said.

"What?" I said, wiping the sweat off my forehead. Suddenly the world seemed ultrasurreal. "What did you say?" I repeated. Time sped up, then it slowed down. Hiro was getting massacred.

"Don't tell her that!" Hiro shouted at the ninjas.

"Why?" the silvery-voiced ninja asked him. "It's true, isn't it? You were to bring her to Kabukicho so that someone could kill her."

"Liar!" I screamed.

Wachter let out a shriek. I wheeled around. The ninja who'd tackled him now wielded a knife. I saw blood. A giant gash opened on Wachter's leg. It looked like they'd sliced open an artery.

I scrambled to get up. "Liar!" I said again to the silvery-voiced ninja. He still giggled at me. I punched him in the face. But he was like a punching bag. He bounced back, still giggling. He unleashed a gigantic knife and started whipping it around toward my face. I backed off, yet managed to trip him up with some low kicks. The knife flew from his hand and landed blade down in the grass. I grabbed it and hefted it over my head.

"It's true," purple sash said. I whipped my head around. He had Hiro in a headlock. "Uyemoto here was basically ordered to kill you. And he didn't carry out his duty."

I looked at Hiro. "Is this *true*?" I screamed. I felt them closing in on me from behind. I whipped around and round-house kicked two ninjas at once. My anger and disbelief manifested in pure kicking power. I saw blood spew from both their noses as they clutched their faces in pain.

Purple sash still had Hiro in a headlock. "He's a traitor," he said. "He's trash."

I looked in Hiro's face for a sign that this wasn't true. But I could see that he was struggling to breathe. I didn't know what to do. *They're making this up,* I thought. *They're making this up so I won't help him.*

I began to pound purple sash's back. I kicked him, trying to trip him up. I wanted him to let go of Hiro. But he still had him in a stranglehold.

And then a blinding crack came to the back of my head. I saw stars—literally. I spun around, a feeling of nausea creeping into my throat. The pain was immense. Blindly I fought for something to hold on to. More kicks came to my side.

And then I got my sight back. I quickly crawled behind a bush. The ninjas, for the moment, had turned back to Hiro. Now he was on the ground. They kicked him with their heels from all angles. Hiro sputtered and spewed gasps and grunts of pain.

Fear overtook me. *Get up, Hiro!* I thought. Why was he being so *weak*? He'd taken on more than one guy before. I tried to push myself up, but my elbows buckled. I was wiped. I lay there, powerless, watching the horrible scene unfold.

Oh my God oh my God. More grunts and sounds of pain came from Hiro. And then for a few seconds the air cleared. The kicking stopped.

"Heaven!" he called weakly. His breath came out uneven and raspy. "Are you there?"

"Yes," I said, thinking that as soon as I called out, the ninjas would be on top of me again. But none of them were.

"Well, then *run*! Get out of here! They're going to kill you next!" he said, mustering all the strength he could.

"No!" I said. What was he talking about? A samurai doesn't run.

I slowly pushed myself up, wincing at the pain in my elbow. As soon as I saw Hiro's face, nausea overtook me again. His cheeks and chin were a bloody, pulpy mess. *I should run,* I thought. *I should get the hell out of here.* This wasn't an I'm-gonna-scare-you attack. This was serious.

They were massacring him.

"Run!" Hiro said again.

"No!" I said. I couldn't leave him.

"Dammit! Just go! This is my seppuku! It must be this way!"

Seppuku. Ritual suicide. Wait. Ritual *suicide*?

What? I said in my mind. I didn't have the strength to scream and knew Hiro didn't have the strength to answer. *Why* would Hiro mention seppuku? *Why* was he just accepting this? Why wasn't he putting up a real fight?

And then I realized.

Ritual suicide. Honor to your superiors.

It was true.

Hiro really *had* been sent to capture me. To kill me.

On unsteady legs, I felt like the wind had been knocked out of me. I leaned over and threw up into the bush. Dizziness overtook me. I took small, cautious breaths, my eyes unfocusing, my body shaking. *It was true.* He'd probably been trying to steer me into a bad section of Kabukicho, where some assailant would pop out of an alley and chop my head off. I stepped back from Hiro, nearly tripping over Wachter's unconscious body. I looked down; his leg had bled profusely. The smell of blood brought another wave of nausea to my throat.

The ninjas continued to beat Hiro. I backed up farther. Hiro had been sent to capture me. Hiro had been sent to kill me. How could this be true? But it must be.

Dazed, in shock, I saw Hiro standing in front of me, bloodless.

You know your enemy now, he said.

Yes, I do.

I am your enemy.

I was thrown back into the present. The grass was ultragreen, rain forest frog green. The light refracting off the windows made my head hurt. I licked my lips and grabbed my jaw. With a final groan Hiro dropped like a boulder to the ground. The ninjas backed up. I could smell blood and death. I breathed heavily.

"No!" I screamed. My voice was the ragged sound of shattering glass.

Hiro managed to turn his head around. Our eyes met. His lips parted slightly. They were covered in dried, black-red blood. "I'm sorry," he croaked. "I tried to explain. I wanted you to know. I thought . . . haragei . . . I thought you could see. . . ."

"But . . . ," I whispered.

"I love you," he murmured before going completely limp.

I screamed. Then for what seemed like both one minute and ten hours, I didn't know what happened. I saw the ninjas back away from Hiro and turn to me. But the next thing I knew, I was running like a crazy person down Imperial Beach Boulevard, still screaming. I ran until I hit the ocean. They weren't behind me. And then I ran into the water, washing off the blood, half delirious. I sat down and let the waves crash over my head. Still wailing and screaming and crying.

I ran for my life.

1 0

I sat in my hotel room, muttering to myself, not knowing what to do. I broke down and called a trauma center finally, two days later. But even then I couldn't explain. "My, um, ex-boyfriend died," I said to the voice on the other end. "In an attack."

"Like a gang attack?" the therapist said.

"Sort of," I said. "But . . . the thing is, he was . . . he was in another gang. A rival gang. He was actually out to get me. Or so they say."

"Wow," the trauma center person said. "Let's focus on the killing. Are you in danger right now?"

"Most likely," I said. "They could come looking for me next."

"No, I mean suicide," she said. "Are you in danger of suicide?"

The mention of suicide made me start bawling again. I felt betrayed, I felt bereaved, and I felt more lost than ever.

I even felt guilty for having been so standoffish to Hiro during our final day together, although I realized that this was idiotic. *He* was the one who'd screwed *me* over.

"I think you should come for a counseling session," the trauma center woman said after I stopped crying.

But I was too afraid to go in and talk to someone I didn't know. How had they found us? Had they followed us the whole way here? But how was that *possible*?

Hiro had been sent to *kill me*?

My instincts, back when Hiro had found me at Masato's, had been right. My haragei. I wondered if Hiro had wanted me to learn haragei in order to realize that he was into things that weren't good without him actually having to *tell* me so. I put my head in my hands and rocked back and forth, suspended in disbelief.

I felt like I was back on that ship. Every time I stood up, I was woozy and either threw up or had to lie down. I'd had very few moments of lucidity during the past two days. Mostly I just stayed in bed, eating nothing, stunned. Weird images of everyone I knew kept floating through my head. I had horrible, sickly dreams; often I woke up screaming.

After I hung up the phone, I heard pounding on my door. My head shot up.

I managed to get up and not barf as soon as I stood. I hobbled over to the door. I hadn't showered since before the fight. My ocean bath didn't count. I smelled like seaweed and sweat.

Through the little peephole, I saw that it was a harmless-looking woman in a uniform. "Housekeeping," she said. "This room hasn't been cleaned for a while." She shoved the Do Not Disturb sign in my face. "I want to change your sheets."

I couldn't open the door for her. "I'm okay," I croaked. I heard her sniffing and walking away.

I sat on my bed. I felt a little better today, a little clearer. My insides were still destroyed, and I was still intensely paranoid and disturbed. But I realized I had to get out of this hotel room. I had to go somewhere else. Those ninjas might have been hired specifically to kill Hiro—but they surely would report back to whoever had sent them that I was still alive. And a new slew of ninjas would be ready to get me at any time. In fact, I was surprised they hadn't struck yet.

I breathed in and out. Okay. I had to move again. Who could I go to? Who did I know in California? Wachter. Dr. Clarkson. But he didn't seem like the type who would take me in. Who else? Cheryl. But I'd never go back to her. She was ready to kill me. Karen. Ugh.

I put my face in my hands and let out a gigantic shudder. My eyes were shriveled up from so much crying; my throat was raw. There was no one. My life was empty. I might as well just offer myself up to the slaughter.

Ritual suicide. Oh God, Hiro. Not you, too.

Teddy.

I rooted through my stuff—noticing Hiro's bag in the process, which again threw me into a crying, near nervous breakdown. I dug out Teddy's number. It was so weathered and old that I had to squint to see the numbers.

Teddy could help me.

I breathed out as if I were living through a straw. With shaking fingers I dialed his number. It rang, then went to voice mail.

"Yo yo, this is Teddy Yukemura, otherwise known as T-Yu. Leave your digits if you're bootilicious; leave nothin' if you're a dog."

Teddy never changed his message. But I couldn't leave a voice mail. I was too terrified. What if someone else had his phone? I hung up.

The sound of his gangsta voice filled me with nostalgia. *God,* I thought. *Even though Teddy's a thug, he would never, ever accept a contract to capture and kill me.*

Then again, I'd never thought Hiro would, either. A lump rose in my throat. My imagination kept getting the best of me. I kept thinking of Hiro, propositioned by Mieko and Masato, agreeing, shaking hands. It was enough to make me rush to the toilet again, throwing up the nonexistent contents of my stomach.

I took a few deep breaths, and the feeling passed.

I stepped out onto the hotel room's balcony, finally taking in the outside world. *Hiro's dead,* I thought. I wondered what had happened to the body. I'd slept with him, and now his body could be decaying on the grass in that apartment complex. I swallowed hard. I wondered if anyone knew. Masato. Mieko.

And then I looked down and saw something really weird.

In the park across the street. Standing cagily behind a tree. Looking up at my window. It was the same cell phone

167

guy. The one who had been standing in front of the police station, the one who had said, "Kaori." I froze. One of his tattoos looked familiar. It was a large, outstretched dragon.

Where had I seen that before?

And his voice. There was something super-familiar about it. And his hair. I scratched my head.

Finally I realized. It was Yoshitomo. The yakuza guy from Life Bytes—the one I'd flirted with in order to get information on my father. I drew in my breath.

What was he doing in San Diego?

I strained to listen to the conversation he was having on the phone. It was hard because he was across the street. I could only hear snippets: "Yes . . . no. I don't know where he is. . . . Had to do a deal up in Santa Cruz for two days. . . . I mean . . . El Penguino . . . Goin' in there now . . . No way . . . *dead?* . . . You're *kidding.* . . . There was already a hit? . . . *Shit* . . . When? . . . Who? . . . Not Takeda, though . . . Okay . . . yeah, maybe I'll call him. . . ."

He paused and glanced up at my room again. I scurried inside, behind the drapes.

He must have been talking about Hiro.

Had he been *part* of the attack?

But then he'd mentioned Takeda. Teddy.

I stood behind the door, breathing in and out. Had he seen me? Was he in cahoots with Kaori? If I was right and he'd been talking about Hiro's death, it sounded like he was just finding out about it. Which meant he hadn't been in on the ninja hit.

Which meant . . . what?

I had to do something. I had to get out of here.

I creaked out of the hotel room, still in my clothes from a week ago, woozy from lack of food and sleep. I passed the maid and her cart. She was cleaning a room two doors down. She looked up at me, opened her mouth to speak, but then stepped back, almost in fear.

I took the fire stairs down to the lobby and crept through a side door. I came out on a side street and looked to my left. The park. I slid along the wall of the hotel and eased behind a Dumpster to shield myself from view.

But when I crept up and peered over the Dumpster, the park was empty. The trees swayed and the leaves kicked up in the breeze. No one on the park bench. No one behind any of the trees. He'd been right there less than a minute ago.

Suddenly I felt the back of my neck prickle. A freakish thought occurred to me: What if Hiro wasn't dead? What if that had all been a setup? And what if this was a setup within that setup? What if someone was behind me, waiting to kill me?

I whirled around, my fists clenched, my leg lifted halfway off the ground, ready to kick.

No one.

I came out of my fighting stance. The street was empty. The park was empty. Maybe I was losing my mind. The wind picked up again and blew my hair around.

"Hello?" a voice echoed behind me.

I jumped about a mile and turned, my fists raised again.

"No!" called out a woman in a maid's uniform. She had just stepped out of the side door to have a cigarette.

"Oh," I said, letting my arms fall to my sides. "I'm sorry. I thought you were . . ."

She looked at me as if I was crazy and then lit the cigarette.

"You hiding from someone?" she said.

"No," I said slowly. I looked to the park again. He was
gone. And then I squinted. There was a smoldering cigarette lying on the ground, half crushed. So he *had* been
here. Or someone that looked just like him. I slumped and
turned and went back inside. The maid gave me one more
look, then exhaled three perfect smoke rings.

"I'm checking out."

There was a new woman at the desk. She was a skinny
girl in her early twenties who had about twenty piercings on
her face. "There a problem?" she said.

"No," I said. "Just hurry."

"Whatever," she said, tallying up my bill.

I'd found another place not too far away that was
equally seedy and cheap. I knew it was a temporary stall. If
Yoshitomo was coming for me next, it wouldn't take him too
long to figure out I'd split and find out where I'd gone. But
then, why hadn't he come and killed me already? I'd been in
the room for days, doing nothing. A perfect target.

Unless he'd wanted Hiro and Hiro alone.

Still, I had to get out of here. I rushed out of my old
room, stuffing Hiro's bag down the garbage chute. I'd considered bringing it along with me, but then thought, *No. You
have to make a clean break*. I took all the money he had in
the bag, plus a couple of bos and his little penlight.
Although the penlight was useful, I couldn't help wanting

something a little personal that had been his. All of his clothes, toiletries, random papers, anything else—gone.

I walked quickly to the new motel, staying in the shade, looking behind me every so often, trying not to seem nervous. I didn't notice anyone following me. I approached the new motel, El Rancho, which had a cheesy swimming pool in the front with a big plastic slide. I rushed into the lobby and got my key. Watching as the bugs skittered into the cracked walls as I snapped on the light, sitting down on the old bed, I felt utterly and desperately alone.

I needed to call someone. I needed to talk. I had a weird, nagging feeling that Hiro was still alive somehow, but I didn't know how that could be. A little voice inside me whispered, *You're just overparanoid.* But he had, after all, been set up to kill me.

I would never, *ever* get over that. Even the thought of it made my world turn upside down.

I tried Katie in Vegas, but the line was busy. I tried some kids from the dojo, but I couldn't get through to them. I even tried to reach a couple of kids from Vibe, but the guy who answered the phone there said they weren't working that night.

"Karen," I whispered. Fat chance Karen would help me. But it was possible that she'd at least listen. Wasn't that what I really needed? Who knew, maybe she'd hear my story, sympathize, and offer help somehow.

I dialed the familiar number. A sinking feeling swirling in my stomach. Before I could hang up, she answered in a rough voice.

"It's Heaven Kogo," I said.

"You," she said after a long pause. "I can't believe you're even calling me."

"Look, Karen, I had nothing to do with—"

"God, you just don't know when to quit, do you? Why don't you just leave me alone? And you know, if it weren't for *you*, he'd still be alive."

I gasped. "So . . . then . . . you know?"

"Of course I know," she said huffily. "It's been all over the news, you moron. Where have you been?"

"I've been *grieving*!" I said. I took a deep breath. "Wait. Let's start over. I had nothing to do with Hiro's death."

"Sure, sure," she said. "You're like a death sentence." She cackled.

"Karen, come on, be rational," I said. "We're both hurt by this, and I think it would do us some good to talk."

"Oh," she said, her voice turning sweet. "And I suppose next you want to suggest we become friends or something?"

"Well, yeah, maybe . . . ," I said.

"I don't think so," Karen said. "Why the hell would I want to be friends with you? You've ruined my life!"

"I . . . ," I sputtered.

"Hiro wasn't even really *interested* in you, anyway," Karen said. "All he was interested in was his little battle against the yakuza. You were its pinup queen. You were its prize. And really, it was so dumb because Hiro was fighting against something that he would eventually *return* to once his money ran out. . . ."

"What?" I said sharply.

Karen stopped.

"What are you talking about, he'd *return* to the yakuza?" I said. "How did you *know* about that?"

"What, you *didn't* know?" Karen said. She started laughing. "Oh, poor Heaven. Oh, this makes my day. He didn't *tell* you, did he! He didn't tell you that his whole *family* is involved and that he was *nothing* like who he said he was. God, we used to talk about it all the time!"

"H-He told me," I stammered.

"Yeah, probably right before he died," Karen said. "Oh God, you're *so* pathetic, Heaven. Get a life, why don't you?"

"Go to hell," I said, full of anger. "You're making all of this up. He never told you any of this."

I hung up, breathing heavily.

When it came to Hiro, everywhere I turned, there was betrayal. All this time Karen had known his background, yet he hadn't told me. I grabbed a pillow from the bed and ripped the pillowcase off and started pulling out the down, fluff by fluff, angrily tearing.

"*Every*thing our relationship was built on was a lie!" I said through my teeth, tearing and tearing out the down, then punching the pillow, pretending it was Karen's head. Then I pretended it was Hiro's head. I pounded and pounded away, hating him more and more and more. I hated him for being dead; I hated him for being alive.

"You stupid asshole! I hate you, I hate you, I hate you," I said, pounding. Pieces of fluff flew everywhere. Then I didn't know whose face I was bashing in. I didn't know if it was Hiro's, or Masato's, or Mieko's, or even my father's. At one point I even envisioned my own face on the pillow, battering it in, frustrated with myself, wanting all this to just end.

Finally I stopped and looked around. I actually felt okay. Something turned over inside me. I suddenly felt . . . I don't know. Light. Free. Free of Hiro. He was dead. I had to rise up from this. I had to be strong.

I *was* my own sensei. I stood up and raised my fingertips to the ceiling, letting my whole body stretch. I *was* my own strength. All these negative people—Karen, Hiro—I didn't need them. I breathed in and out, conscious of myself finally, for once.

I had to move on. I realized now what I had to do.

I had to find my mother.

Would you believe I found out about Hiro's death on the news? I came home from the dojo—not even strong enough to teach a class anymore—and flopped down on the chair. I felt like crying. And this was before I saw the newscast.

The breakup with Hiro had torn me apart. But it had done something else, too. I had become this vengeful person, and I couldn't stop myself. I couldn't stop these horrible things from pouring out of my mouth. And I couldn't stop obsessing over what Hiro was doing. That one time he'd come into the dojo with Heaven and that stupid haircut of hers. What jerks. Just parading her around, saying, "Look, Karen, look at my new girlfriend, look hard, 'cause you aren't good enough."

So I sat down on the couch and turned on the news and there it was. That yellow banner at the bottom with the headline UNKNOWN MAN FOUND MURDERED. And there was some lawn in San Diego, a newscaster at the scene, yellow police tape, the whisperings of ninja, a Japanese boy without ID.

I knew it was Hiro. I just knew it. They zeroed in on his face (as close as they could get) and there he was. I nearly choked on my tongue.

I sobbed and sobbed and sobbed all night. I knew it was that bitch's fault. She killed him. Somehow she killed him. Such trash. Her family and their yakuza filth. The next day I took a sick day, wallowing in bed, miserable. I writhed around for a while, trying to deal.

And then the phone rang.

And it was her.

I couldn't get away from her!

But it was as if on cue. In a way, I was waiting for her call. I'd known she would call if she was in the States—which I was sure she was. She was right at Hiro's side when the whole thing went down, I bet. Yet she's still alive. And he's dead.

I really threw her for a loop when I mentioned all that yakuza stuff. I made a lot of it up. I didn't really know if Hiro's whole family was involved, although I'd definitely suspected something like that was up. I mean, who cares about the yakuza and avenging and stopping it unless you're not tied to it somehow? Heaven's such a moron. A monkey could have made that deduction. Leave it to Hiro to ditch me for some dumb girl with a mobster father.

But I really stunned her, and then as I heard her catch her breath, I realized: it's true. Hiro really was involved with the yakuza. He must have told Heaven that, and she's pissed because she thinks I knew first. The whole thing felt delicious and horrible at the same time. Delicious because Heaven now questions her relationship with Hiro. But horrible because I know the truth—he told her far more than he told me.

Her gasp was priceless, though. But now, shit. Where has all this gotten me? What will I do now? I still have no idea what will become of my life. I still don't know if I'll ever get my strength back, if I'll ever be able to turn things around. Will I ever meet someone new? Someone who . . . isn't Hiro? Who is as far from Hiro as you can get?

There's one thing for sure. If I have anything to do with it, I'll never see Heaven Kogo again.

Karen

1 1

I sat in the lotus pose for a little while, trying to breathe calmly. Then I called the San Diego police station.

"Yes, is Detective Wachter available?" I said to the voice that answered.

"Who is this?" the person barked.

"Um . . . ," I said. "Is Detective Wachter there?"

"He's in the hospital," she said tersely.

"Oh . . . which one?" *He's alive,* I thought gratefully.

"Who *is* this?"

"Is he hurt badly?"

"He might not make it through the night. Good-bye."

Click.

I sat for a moment, blinking in the half darkness. The sun reflected all the dust that was constantly swirling around the room.

So I would have to go it alone.

I had a list and a map and I was ready. I figured I'd just

hit the remaining houses on foot. The ones that were too far, I'd figure out for later. As I walked to the first house, I stayed guarded, still on the lookout for Yoshitomo. I half expected ninjas to drop from the sky, but they didn't.

The first house I got to looked nice enough; I could see a marble swimming pool in the backyard. Standing at the front door, I felt a twinge. Hiro had been so eager to help me with this search. Did I feel him standing with me right now? But I didn't. I felt Ohiko standing with me more than I felt Hiro.

I rang the doorbell.

A woman appeared. "Can I help you?" she asked.

"I'm . . . I'm Heaven Kogo," I said.

"Uh-huh," she said. She had graying hair and a nice, friendly face, but she looked nothing like me. I thought my mom would be a little younger, too.

I hemmed and hawed around the issue for a little bit, and then finally blurted, "Did you give a baby up for adoption twenty years ago?"

She looked at me like I'd lost my mind. "Uh, no," she said.

"I'm sorry," I said. "I probably just sounded like a crazy person right then. I'm a little stressed. I have this list of names of people who might potentially be my birth mother, and . . ."

"And I'm on the list?" the woman said, amused. She smiled—her face was open and friendly. "That's hilarious, because I've never had any children. I'm a lesbian."

"Oh," I said.

"I wonder how I got on the list," she said. "That's fascinating."

I began to tell her about the biometrics and Dr. Clarkson. She seemed enthralled. "I'm a journalist," she said. "This would make a fascinating story. Would you mind if I put this in the *San Diego Union-Tribune* Science section?"

"Um . . . ," I said. "How about when my search is over? I'll contact you." I pointed to my list. "I have your number."

She smiled again, and I stepped off the porch. That was all I needed: my name plastered in the paper. Doofus Heaven goes looking for her birth mom. Wouldn't Mieko have gotten a kick out of that?

It was easy to get to the next woman's house on foot. I wandered through the cute Gaslight district. Lots of restaurants and shops called out to me, but I realized I didn't have much desire to get into anything. I was so far from being shopaholic Heaven of Tokyo that it was scary. *I'm growing up,* I thought. *Those things don't matter anymore.*

I passed a dojo and felt a longing. I could see people on the second floor kicking and going through punching drills. I wanted to go inside. *Maybe when all this is over,* I thought.

Suddenly something caught my eye across the street. A guy in a leather jacket, talking on a cell phone.

Yoshitomo!

I ran haphazardly across the street and tailed him around the corner. He seemed to be walking with purpose. I tried to hear his conversation, but I was too far away. I crept a little closer. He went into a coffee shop and stood at the counter, still chattering on his phone.

I hung in the alley next to the coffee shop, trying to practice my shinobi-iri. The shadows were very deep and long,
so it didn't seem like he saw me. When he got his coffee
and looked like he was going to be leaving soon, I flattened
myself against the wall, waiting for him to pass.

And then a hand over my mouth.

"Don't move," said a voice. I felt something cool and
metal press against my cheek. Where had this person come
from? The alley must have been deeper than I'd thought.

"Give me your wallet," the guy barked.

"I don't have my wallet," I said.

"What do you have?" he asked.

With shaking fingers I found my bag over my shoulder.
The guy snatched it away. I heard him rustling through it
with one hand.

I have to get out of here, I thought.

"Aha!" he said, his hands on something. He pulled out
the snaky, sparkling links of Masato's diamond necklace.

"No!" I said. I hadn't pawned it yet. I hadn't had the
time. The guy closed his fist tightly around it, the gun still at
my forehead. Quickly I pressed my elbow against his solar
plexus. The gun clattered to the ground. Next I kneed him in
the groin.

"Jesus!" he cried, stepping back in agony.

I grabbed his hand, but he wouldn't let go of the necklace. "I need that!" I said through clenched teeth. We wres-
tled for a few moments. He wouldn't loosen his grip. Finally
I bit his hand. My teeth sank in hard.

That did the trick. He screamed. His hand instinctively

opened. I snatched the jewels and punched him in the face. Then I ran into the light, smack into Yoshitomo.

"Oof!" I said, wheeling backward.

Yoshitomo took a look at me, completely bowled over. I had the jewels dangling in one hand, my bag in the other. The mugger groaned and spit in the darkness.

"Hey," Yoshitomo said slowly. He was wearing the same leather jacket. He also had big, thick, black studded cuffs around his wrist. Painted on the cuffs were three angry-looking dragons. The detail was incredibly intricate and a little scary. I'd never seen anything like it. On his hand, between his thumb and his pointer finger, was a tattoo that said KAORI. I blinked, completely shocked, trying to regain my composure.

Then he straightened up, smiled, and took a step forward.

But I didn't let him. I kicked him in the crotch as hard as I could. Then I turned on my heels and ran as far and fast as possible. And when I'd gone a ways, I turned back. He hadn't followed me.

Idiot, I told myself. *Why did you let him see you? But what should I have done? Stood there and let that mugger rob me of the only thing I have that might be worth some money?*

It had gotten to the point where I was talking to myself. I was feeding myself both sides of the argument.

After running and running and running, I calmed down. I was far enough away. I had to summon my haragei awareness. I had to be very careful. I still planned on continuing my search, but I had to realize that the word might get out somehow. I didn't know how connected Yoshitomo was. It sounded like he didn't have any idea that Hiro had been killed until the other day. But then . . . how did he know Kaori? Were they planning some secret operation themselves? Was there a bounty out on Hiro's and my heads through the yakuza? Was it every man for himself when it came to hunting down and killing us?

But that didn't make sense. The guys the other day had killed only Hiro. They hadn't really been interested in me.

So . . . what was Yoshitomo *doing*?

He'd mentioned Teddy in that phone conversation. They were friends. Was he just . . . spying?

If I kept up this line of thought, my head would be tied in knots. I had to press on. I looked at my list. The next woman's house was, freakishly enough, in the neighborhood where our fight had been. Great. As soon as I saw some familiar streets, I froze. Was it safe to walk around here? I looked right and left. I looked for fire trucks or police cars or something. What had the scene been like when they'd found Hiro's body? I shuddered.

Please don't let Yoshitomo be in cahoots with Mieko. . . .

Still, the house wasn't too close to where the fight had been, so I walked on. I kept thinking I heard footsteps behind me. I'd stop, turn, but no one would be there. Or it would be a sprinkler, or a car, or a kid on a bike.

A man answered the door at the house. I launched into a more poised version of my monologue: "Hi, I'm looking

for someone named . . ." I consulted my list. "Amelia Saki."
A Japanese name! Could this be her?

The man frowned. "Why?" he asked.

"I want to ask her some questions." I smiled.

He clammed up and started to shut the door.

"Hey!" I said. "Wait! I might be her daughter! Did she give a child up for adoption about twenty years ago?"

"No. That's impossible," the guy barked. "And besides, she's dead. You can't ask her anything anyway."

I went down the steps. What if she had been my mother? What if . . . what if someone had had her killed?

But there was something about the house and the man and just . . . everything that made me think I wasn't related to these people at all. I didn't know if I should trust my instincts, but something was telling me to move on.

I wandered back through the Gaslight district and found myself in front of the dojo again. I stared at it. The first-floor lobby area had artful tigers and dragons and other jungle scenes painted on the walls. The studios looked clean and new and white. A girl sat at the front desk, talking on the phone. Karen used to do the reception job sometimes.

Karen.

Ugh.

Why in the world had I reached out to her? Hadn't I learned my lesson?

I looked at my list, weary. There were so many names, and so many of them were on the outskirts of town or places like Oceanside or Chula Vista. I didn't have any idea how I'd get there unless I took the bus specifically for that purpose.

I was running out of money. I was running out of time.

I realized I could probably call a lot of these out-of-town names back at the hotel and get an idea of what they were all about. There was only one more name on the list whose address was close by. A woman named Sara Armstrong.

I followed the directions on my map and came to a windswept, cozy street by the beach. The sun had sunk low in the sky, and I heard kids laughing not far away. I found the house—it was quaint, with a great garden in the front. Sara Armstrong had an Audi TT. *Nice wheels,* I thought.

Something about the house seemed to be inviting to me, in the same way the dojo had been. *I've seen this house,* I thought. But I didn't know where. I'd never been on this street before. I'd only been to San Diego once, for no time at all. How could I have seen it?

I trudged up the stairs. No doubt this Sara person would be a cranky old woman or another lesbian or dead. This probably wasn't even her house.

I rang the doorbell. I heard footsteps. A petite woman opened the door. She had pale skin, brownish hair, fine bones, and a pleasant-looking face. She wore simple white drawstring pants and an old, thrift-shop-style T-shirt that had a big number 23 on it. *Too young,* I thought. Still . . .

I studied her carefully. She studied me.

"Yes?" the woman asked. Her voice was familiar. Her face was familiar. *I've seen this face,* I thought. *I've seen this house. Where? Where?*

"I'm . . . ," I started. "I'm Heaven."

The woman looked at me. Her lips parted. A wave of

disbelief rolled over her face. "*What* did you say your name was?"

"Heaven," I said. "Heaven Kogo."

She seriously looked like she was going to lose it. "Don't shut the door," I said, hoping she wouldn't turn me away.

"I wasn't going to," she said. She couldn't stop looking at me. All of a sudden she pulled me inside. She stood back to look at me again.

"M-Mom?" I blurted.

Tears came to her eyes. "Is it really you?" she asked. "You are . . . you are Heaven?"

"Yes," I said. I couldn't believe it. This was her. This was my mother.

"I never thought I'd find you," she said, and hugged me ever so tight.

12

We didn't say anything for a bit but instead just hugged and cried. The whole situation was a little weird. It felt surreal. *I'm not here,* I thought. *But yes, I am. This is happening.*

Finally we both settled down. Sara stood back from me and smiled. "It's just so unbelievable," she said.

"I know," I said.

"Come on inside," she said. She led me into the front room of her house, which was bathed in light. The floors were pale wood. There were two luxurious leather chairs and a sleek coffee table. Somewhere I could hear the sound of water falling. The walls were pretty spare but painted a very calming shade of green.

"It's so calm in here," I said.

"It's my little oasis," she said. She turned to me again, still breathless. "You're taller than me," she said. She started laughing. I could see a lot of my facial characteristics—my nose, my cheekbones, my jawline—also in her face. She wasn't Japanese but looked exotic in some way.

"This is so amazing," I said. I realized how happy I was. I felt like I was really, truly coming home. I noticed a big fish tank in the corner full of black-and-white fish. I wondered if I should sit down.

"You really don't understand," Sara said, tearing up again. "I've wanted to contact you for so long now. But I wasn't able to."

"You knew where I was?" I said. "I thought I was just . . . I don't know . . . given up for adoption, the way it's normally done."

Sara shook her head. "No," she said. "There's more to it than that." She kept breathing in and taking sweeping looks at all of me, and then clapping her hand over her mouth, amazed.

"I wanted to find you for years," she said. "But when I let you go, Konishi said that I must never see you again. He said that if I tried, he would have to take drastic measures." She swallowed hard.

"Whoa, whoa, hold up!" I said. "You *know* Konishi?"

Sara sighed. "Yes."

I stared at her. "How?"

Sara took a deep breath. "He really told you nothing, didn't he? Maybe it's just as well. Heaven, Konishi is your real father."

"What?" I barely whispered it.

"You better sit down for this," she said. "Do you want anything? Tea?"

"No, thanks," I said, sinking into one of the leather chairs. I had a heavy feeling in my chest, like my universe was about to unravel again.

Sara sat down opposite me. "Okay. Where to start? So I was working as a stewardess on JAL. God, I've wanted to tell you this story ever since I can remember!" She paused, wiping her eyes, grabbing a Kleenex from the coffee table and blowing her nose.

"Sorry if it seems like I'm losing it here," she said.

"Believe me, I understand," I said, feeling a little teary myself.

"Anyway, I was a stewardess. Those were the golden days of working for the airlines. . . . I'd never do it nowadays. I met Konishi because he took a lot of international and transcontinental flights. He was married, of course, but I didn't know that at the time. And he even had a little son that I didn't know about until later."

"Ohiko," I whispered.

"I was his favorite stewardess, or so he said. He requested that I be on every one of his flights. And then slowly we got into a relationship," Sara said. "He was a wonderful man. But I didn't know anything about him, of course. I was young—only twenty. I didn't know what I was doing. I just thought it was exciting. This handsome, rich Japanese businessman was interested in me.

"But then I got pregnant. With you. And Konishi . . . he lost it. 'This can't be happening,' he said, 'You must get an abortion.'"

"He *did*?" I said.

"I'm sorry if any of this gets too difficult. We can stop whenever."

"Are you crazy?" I said. "I want to know this. I *need* to know this."

She took another deep breath. "He wanted me to have an abortion because he didn't want it to come out that he had an illegitimate child. I told him that I would keep it a secret with my life; I really wanted this baby. I wanted you. I didn't want to give you up." Tears sprang from her eyes again.

"Go on," I said. Out of the corner of my eye I noticed a big yellow cat walk slowly around the corner.

"He said that wasn't possible. Too many people would try to find out. 'Why?' I asked. At first I thought maybe he was a politician or something. You know how the media in this country are about politicians and famous people and their affairs. Maybe this happened in Japan, too. But then I found out what he did. That he was . . . that he was the boss . . . of . . ."

"Yeah," I said.

"Finally we agreed that I could have the baby as long as I would give you up after you were born. Konishi would 'adopt' you as a charity case. He basically was afraid that I'd squawk some years down the line. Which I wouldn't have."

"But maybe you would've," I said. "What if you'd needed money? That kind of benefactor is tempting."

"He paid me," Sara said, biting her lip. "He paid me to keep my mouth shut. I mean, it wasn't that I wanted to *be* with him. . . . I just wanted you."

I thought for a moment. I remembered Hiro saying that

he'd seen documents in his father's house that listed *female, San Diego,* and then a sum of money.

I thought of something else, too. "This means that Konishi cheated on Mieko," I said, leaning back into the couch.

"That's his wife, right? Yes, I have a feeling she's always known. I don't know how he really introduced you into the family. I mean, yes, there was the plane crash and he 'rescued' you, but he was going to do it differently. I'm sure Mieko was very confused about all that."

"So what about the crash?" I asked.

"Okay, I'm getting to that. I was pregnant with you, and I figured, too bad, Konishi, I'll have this baby and then I'll go into hiding. I had some friends in backwoods Canada who agreed to hide me for a while so he wouldn't know where to find me. So that was my plan. I certainly didn't want you to be raised as the daughter of a yakuza kingpin. Konishi and I had horrible arguments about it all the time. He wanted nothing to do with me by the time I was about six months pregnant with you. But he *coveted* you. Come hell or high water, he was getting you and raising you on his own."

"Wow," I said.

"As I approached my ninth month of pregnancy, Konishi started hounding me about the 'arrangements.' I even had a couple of 'visits' from his thugs, muscling me, reminding me of my 'task' I was to perform once I'd delivered and nursed you. I was supposed to raise you to a certain point—wean you off breast milk, basically—and then someone would come to collect you. I was so scared of those thugs who kept banging on my door at the weirdest hours of the night that I was afraid I'd miscarry or you'd be born with a complex or something." She laughed softly. "Remember, I was only twenty years old."

"My age," I said. "Or almost."

"That's right," she said gently. "In a couple of weeks."

We looked at each other. "So April 8 *is* my real birthday."

"Yes," she said, smiling. "I'm glad he kept it that day."

The big yellow cat walked into the room and jumped onto Sara's lap. I reached out to pet him and he immediately began to purr. "He likes you," Sara said. "His name is Sam."

We sat there for a moment, soaking all of this in. Sara had a couple of prisms hanging from the window; they made rainbow patterns on the floor.

"Anyway. Soon enough I went into labor, and I went to the hospital. My mom took me, I remember. My mom was actually very supportive of the pregnancy, even if she didn't completely approve of it."

"Your mom?" I said. "My grandmother?"

"Well, yes, that's right. Of course." She smiled.

"Does she still live around here?"

"She lives in Orange County," Sara said.

"God, I have a grandmother," I said. "Konishi's parents were dead." I paused. Konishi was my father. Oh. My. God.

"Anyway, as soon as I delivered you—I didn't even have time to nurse you or anything—you were gone. One of his henchmen came and took you away. They must have paid off all the doctors and nurses, because they heavily sedated me, and the next thing I remember, I was lying at home in my bed with a private nurse by my side. Konishi must have paid for it all."

"What did your mom think?" I asked.

"My mom doesn't talk about it," Sara said sadly. "It was a terrible day. For weeks after, I would scream. I hated Konishi. And then one day I thought, wait. I can go to the police about this. This is ridiculous. I can't let this man ruin my life. This is my baby, too. But as soon as I had that thought—it was so eerie—my phone rang. It was Konishi himself. 'I've been thinking,' he said, 'that you might be considering going to the police. But that is a very bad move. Even if you would sacrifice your life, do you want to sacrifice your daughter's?'

"Something about it made me think he'd harm *you* if I came looking for you. I was terrified. So I didn't call the police. Then I had another idea. I could get someone to smuggle you out of Japan. I had got wind of what Konishi's 'plan' was going to be—a stewardess had spied for me while he spoke to one of his henchmen on a business flight back to Tokyo. Basically, to make it look like he'd 'rescued' you, they were going to plant you in an adoption agency at first, and Konishi, out of kindness, would take pity on you and take you home. His wife would ask later, 'Why so spur of the moment?' And he'd say, 'I just took one look at her and I couldn't resist.'"

"As *if* Mieko would accept that," I said. "That's the lamest thing I've ever heard."

"Well, he needed *some* way to get you into the house

without admitting to Mieko that he'd had an affair," Sara said, downtrodden.

"Even though she probably knew anyway," I said, petting the cat's back. "I wonder if that's why she hates him so much."

"He never spoke of her," Sara said, her eyes looking off into the distance.

"But anyway," she continued. "I found out which orphanage they were holding you in for a day and paid off a couple of people to steal you from there and fly you back to San Diego. Then we were going to go off somewhere where Konishi could never find us. It was very perilous, but I had to get you out of there. I felt that you were in danger."

"God," I said. "I had a nanny, actually. I never even knew my father was involved in any of this until a couple of months ago."

"I'm glad to hear that," Sara said. "Because I was seriously freaking out. Later I wondered if it had something to do with postpartum depression. I assumed the worst was happening to you. But I also missed you. I wanted you back so badly. You were mine. Anyway, these people I knew actually managed to steal you from the orphanage. My friends drove you to the airport, where it was arranged through some of my contacts at JAL that you would sit in a spare first-class seat of a plane leaving for L.A. that night. The stewardesses would take good care of you; one volunteered to sit with you the whole plane ride and carry you on and off the plane."

She cleared her throat. "But then . . . the plane

crashed." I saw her face grow red and sorrowful. "When I found out, I broke down. *My baby is dead*, I thought. *She was better off staying with Konishi.* I didn't think I could ever possibly feel worse than on the day you were taken from me.

"And I didn't even know you were alive for a while. I thought you'd died. The news about the crash and who'd survived and all of that wasn't really disclosed here in the States."

She took a sip of water and looked at me, her eyes wide. "But then I found out you hadn't even boarded the plane."

"What?"

"My friends who snuck you on the plane had reported back to me that you'd gotten on okay. But then I didn't hear from any of those friends again. And then it got back to me through some other people I know in Japan that my friends were killed immediately after calling me and telling me that you were safe."

"By Konishi," I said.

"Yes. He found out what was going on and made them call me and say everything was fine. Then he killed them, took you back, and . . . well . . . I think this is what happened . . . did something to the aircraft to crash the plane and make it *seem* like, at least to me, you were dead. So I'd never come looking for you."

"You're kidding," I said.

"I might be wrong," she said. "I don't want you to have this terrible opinion of your father now, but . . ."

"It's all right," I said. "I need to know all of this. And

believe me, the things I've found out about *everyone* in my life . . ." I shook my head. "But the news reports said there was one survivor."

"Yes, the news reports in *Japan* said that. I think they were manipulated. Which is how Konishi could adopt you, you see? But if you look at the *American* news reports on the same thing, they say no survivors. The news about little Heaven Kogo didn't hit the American papers." She shifted her weight and gestured upstairs. "I have a copy of the *New York Times*, the edition that was published the day after the crash. I'll show it to you. You'll see."

"Wow," I said. "He manipulated the press?"

"I think," Sara said. "I mean, I'm into conspiracies. Maybe I'm biased." She smiled sadly. "But . . . how else could that have happened?"

"Yeah," I said. "Wow. So I've never *been* in a plane crash."

"Nope," Sara said.

"And then he adopted me," I said.

"It was a perfect plan. It was an even easier way to explain it to his wife, I'm sure. I mean, no doubt there were questions. Why would a man bring a baby girl to a perfectly healthy childbearing woman? Why bring a baby who was in a plane crash? Isn't that bad luck? But I don't know. Maybe Mieko didn't ask questions. But there he was, all over the news, before I could even make a move. I got a lot of threatening calls after that. 'If you try anything like that again, your daughter will be the one who suffers.' I had my hands tied behind my back."

She blew her nose. "And when I found this all out—you were probably about four or so—I wanted contact with you. But Konishi was the one with the money and the power and all of Japan's muscle behind him. I was terrified for years that he would blow up my house or just rub me out somehow. I wonder, in some ways, why he's kept me alive all this time. The only thing I can come up with is that he loved me. And he loves you. And he doesn't want to kill the person who gave birth to you."

My eyes filled with tears.

"He *did* care about you," Sara said. "Right?"

"Yes," I said, thinking of my father and what they were doing to him. "He did. He cared very much."

"He cared about me, too. Once." She looked at me. "God, I'm so sorry. I hate to have told you this. I wish it were a simple story—that I gave you up for adoption and Konishi adopted you and that was it. But there's so much more to it."

"There's always more to it when it comes to my life." I groaned, sinking back into the chair, wringing my hands.

"For years I'd wondered about you. God, where is she? I'd think. What is she doing? How is Konishi treating her? But then . . . all this stuff came out about you. Just a few months ago. You were missing, for one. Your wedding was here. There was an attack. I actually even went to L.A. a couple of times to look for you." She sighed. "But, well, I failed. And then I hoped you'd come looking for me. But then . . . how would you know?"

"I didn't find out from my father," I said. "I found out from . . . from my ex-boyfriend."

"And then there was that *song*," Sara said.

"'Heaven's Gone'?" I said. "You know that?"

She nodded. "They play it at the place I work sometimes. We're really into Japanese stuff there. And I have a working knowledge of the language. So when I heard the song—mumbly as it is—I freaked out. Oh my God, they're talking about my daughter? Is any of this stuff true?"

"Most of it wasn't," I said. "I was never locked in a box or a cage or any of that other stuff the song says."

"Oh, I know," Sara said. "It was amazing to hear a song about you. Amazing and scary." She looked at me again. "You know, when I gave birth to you, I didn't have a name picked out. But I really like Heaven."

I smiled. She smiled back.

"So you say you found all this out from your ex-boyfriend?" Sara asked. "Tell me about that. Why is he your ex? Is he still around?"

"It's a long story," I said. "And I don't know if I should call him my ex-boyfriend. He was a friend of my brother's, and I went to him when I fled my wedding in L.A. But . . . he turned out not to be who he seemed. He turned out to be in on a sting to lead me back to Masato and Mieko."

"Who?" she asked.

I thought about this. "God, I have a lot of explaining to do," I said. So I started at the beginning. I told her about my arranged marriage. Teddy. The attack. The ninjas. Ohiko dying. Hiro's house. Karen. The samurai training. Cheryl, the club, the fire. Vegas. Katie. Mexico. Detective Wachter. Japan. My father's danger. The sub. My changed feelings toward Hiro. His death. The search for Sara. It must have taken hours.

Sara was a wonderful listener. She asked questions, she made us tea, and she turned on a few lights as dusk fell. I glanced at my watch and realized we'd been talking for over five hours. And I could have gone on talking for so much longer.

"So Hiro turned against you," she said.

"Yes," I said.

"I'm sorry. But it seems like he agreed to it and then decided not to."

"Yeah," I said. "I mean, there was a moment there when I thought he was trying to pass some code in Kabukicho and stall us there, and maybe that was when it was all going to happen. . . . I don't know. But then he changed his mind."

"So he really didn't turn against you," Sara said.

"Yes, but he did," I said. "He agreed to do it in the first place."

"But," Sara said, "what if he told his father he'd do it and all the while knew that he *wouldn't*? At least by agreeing to do it, he could get out of his house and get on Masato's property, steal you away without Masato waking up, basically capture you for himself."

"Hmmm," I said. "I never thought of that. It was almost as if . . ." I paused to think. "It was almost as if that attack was staged basically to punish Kaori and let me go. I beat her to a pulp."

Sara smiled. "And you said that she set you up in . . . Roppongi, was it? Of course it was a punishment, then.

Masato didn't wake up because he knew that Hiro was stealing you away in order to kill you. If his assistant, who messed up, got hurt in the process, then all the better. He wouldn't have had to lift a finger."

"God, it's so weird," I said. "I wonder if that was Hiro's intent."

"It's hard to say," Sara said. "But if he really loved you, it's a possibility, don't you think?"

"I don't know," I said. "I don't know about anything anymore. And it doesn't matter, anyway. I wouldn't have been happy with Hiro for the rest of my life. I'm stronger than him. I'm my own person. I make mistakes, but at least I'm honest with myself. Hiro . . . Hiro was messed up."

Sara paused, poured some tea, and didn't say anything. Sam was now lying on a small carpet between the kitchen and the living room. I could still hear the sound of water falling. I wondered if she had an installation outside. I wanted to see the rest of the house.

"You've been doing some martial arts, you said?" Sara asked.

"I know," I said. "It's kinda silly."

"Goodness, no," Sara said. "I run a dojo."

"You're kidding."

"No, dead serious. It's in the Gaslight district. In my paranoia about Konishi's thugs coming and knocking down my door, I decided, Girl, you have to get strong. So I started taking judo classes. Then I moved on to aikido and karate. Now I just do everything. I love it. The studio's been open for about eight years, and things are going great. We even

200

have yoga classes in there now. Yoga's all the rage, you know."

I nodded dumbly. "You said the studio is in the Gaslight district?" She nodded. "I've seen it!" I said. "Does it have tigers and stuff painted in the lobby?"

"That's the one," she said.

"God, I could've just walked in and said, 'Hi, I'm Heaven Kogo,' and maybe I would've met you?"

"Maybe," Sara said. "Although I'm usually teaching."

"Still," I said. "Wow. I really wanted to go in there when I saw it." I sat back and looked carefully at her. I hadn't noticed, but she was in great shape. Her arms looked way better than mine.

"This is so cool," I said. "My mother runs a ryu."

"If you want to continue to train, I can help you," she said. "That is, if you think you're going to stay around. . . ."

"Are you kidding?" I said, laughing. "Where would I go?"

"You could stay here of course. Anything for you."

"I would love to," I said. All my dreams were coming true.

"This is home," she said.

It was nearly 1 A.M. I followed Sara into her kitchen, which had a red, antique-looking fridge and pots and pans hanging from every available spot on the wall. It still felt very Zen somehow. She made us hummus and pita and brought out some cold pasta salad and iced tea. I ate ravenously, trying to remember the last time I'd eaten something. I probably looked like skin and bones; since Hiro died, I hadn't eaten anything at all. Which made me remember: I still had to pay my hotel bill. I had to pawn the necklace so I'd have some money. *All in good time,* I thought.

Sara excused herself to go to the bathroom and to give Sam some medicine. I sank back into the couch and tried to assess what we'd talked about. I thought about Hiro. It was true what Sara had said. Even though he had agreed to the task from his father, he hadn't followed through with it. And that should count for something. I didn't have a doubt in my mind that Hiro truly had loved me, right to his death. I sighed. I hoped that he saw me, wherever he was. And I hoped that he was proud.

We went upstairs. "Let me show you the rest of the house," Sara said. There was a spare bedroom that was airy and clean, with pale blue walls and a low, modern-looking wood bed. There were big French movie posters plastered everywhere. A blue iMac sat in the corner. "I can move the computer out of here if you want," she said. "Is this room okay?"

"It's great," I said. "So's the computer."

"Wow," Sara said, stepping back. "It's amazing how things can change in a day. I have a daughter again. After twenty years I have a daughter."

"You've always had a daughter," I said, sitting on the bed.

"That's true," she answered.

There were so many things I still wanted to ask her about. What was *her* life like? Did she have a boyfriend now? Did she have any other children? What did she do for fun? She didn't look forty. She looked more like twenty-five.

We stared at each other, smiling brightly, neither of us really wanting to go to bed.

"Well, I have a toothbrush and stuff you can borrow since all of your things are back at that hotel," she said.

"Okay."

"And tomorrow I have to be at the dojo early, but you can come along if you want."

"That sounds wonderful," I said, lying back on the bed. It was heavenly. There were about five million pillows. The sheets smelled like lavender.

"I'll go get you some towels," Sara said, and turned to leave the room. But then she froze.

Outside, I heard a dog bark crazily. Something about it sounded ominous, intrusive. Sara glanced at me.

Then there was a crack. The sound of splintering wood. Sara whipped around and ran into the hall.

"Oh my God," she whispered.

I jumped out of bed and ran to the window to see what was happening. Thundering feet. Black masks. Swords. Windows breaking. I blinked a couple of times and then my adrenaline started to pump.

Four guys were casing the house. I saw a few skulking behind trees, hiding behind Sara's car.

Ninjas.

Then one of them spotted us upstairs and pointed.

Everyone stood still for a moment.

The ninjas glared up at us, out for blood. One of them, I recognized, had been there for the attack on Hiro.

This clan had to be there on orders from Masato.

203

"It's happening," Sara whispered.

One of the ninjas charged up the stairs.

"How good a fighter are you?" Sara asked, turning to me.

"I can hold my own," I said.

"All right, then," she said. "It's time to show off your stuff."

And we rushed down to meet them.

13

I grabbed a broom as a makeshift bo.

There were four attackers, all dressed in the same weird purple-and-black getup. One of them came toward me quickly, throwing a kick inches from my face.

I retaliated with the bo, striking back. But the attacker wheeled around and kicked me low. I stumbled, falling up the stairs. Something crashed on the other side of the room. Sara was taking on two attackers at once.

I glanced quickly at her. She was *good*. She was much better than Hiro. She was fast, efficient. She knew how to use the shadows, she knew how to use her body, and it seemed like she sized up her opponent's weaknesses instantly.

I pressed myself up and started engaging in hand-to-hand combat with this one attacker who wouldn't leave me alone. He was aggressive, throwing blows to my shoulders and chest. I managed to land one on his nose and felt the bone structure of his face. Even though a mask covered it up, I could feel the face's delicateness. *Weird,* I thought. Usually these attackers had bone structure like the front grille of a Mack truck.

This attacker is smaller than the others, too, I thought amidst quick, choppy blows to the shoulder.

Sara was fiercely pummeling her opponents. Already she'd thrown one into a wall, and he lay crumpled up against it, clearly knocked out. She was working on the other two, whirling and kicking, her limbs swift and fluid.

I seized the bo, feeling like a sluggish elephant. This attacker wouldn't give me any breathing room. Without a minute's pause he'd been kicking or punching some part of me. Already I felt my eye swell up in pain. I tried to block with my body, but I was growing slow. Suddenly I had an idea.

I'd flip him.

He was shorter than the others were; I'd have no trouble with this. I'd flipped men twice his size. Quickly I rammed into his lower legs, planted my feet, and threw him over my shoulder. I heard the wood floor shudder and creak under his weight.

"Whoa," Sara said. She'd dispensed with *three* of the fighters already.

"You're a machine," I whispered, looking at the fighters writhing on the ground.

"Let's not get ahead of ourselves," she said quickly. "Look."

Seven more attackers ran in, fists and weapons flying.

I managed to stave off some of them, whirling and kicking. One snapped my bo in half, and I struggled to find a replacement.

"Use this!" Sara said, pulling something down from the wall. It was a sword.

I caught the sword with one hand. A flash went through me—it was like holding the Whisper of Death. I looked at it closer.

The engraving. It *was* the Whisper of Death.

"How . . . ?" I started.

"I'll explain later," Sara said, out of breath, knocking down man after man with blows to the stomach, to the side of the head. She knocked a knife out of one's hand; it flew haphazardly and landed sideways right in someone's stomach. The attacker shrieked, grabbed his midsection, and dropped like a stone. Blood oozed onto Sara's carpet.

I looked at the Whisper. It felt right in my hands. *It's been returned,* I thought, *to its rightful owner.* I swung it over my head. It felt light. I had control.

The little attacker rose up again. From across the room someone threw him not one sword, but two. Strategically he whirled them over his head. The metal shone and danced quickly, coming inches from my body. I wasn't very skilled in sword fighting. Hiro and I hadn't gotten that far with it yet. I'd have to wing it.

I brandished the Whisper and held it away from my body, blocking the two swords' mighty blows. But the little attacker was relentless. My feet moved endlessly and my ankles ached. The little attacker began to laugh. My blocks became sluggish; he'd nicked the sides of my arms. I could see blood oozing through my shirt.

Come on, Whisper. Please help me now.

"Need a hand?" Sara asked.

I nodded, and Sara moved behind the attacker. I nodded again, and before the attacker could move, Sara grabbed him, wrapping her arms around his stomach. Then she moved her arms up around his neck and put him in a hold, choking him. His grip on the swords slackened. Still, he waved his arms around frantically, slicing the air. I darted to the other side of him and grabbed the swords out of his hands.

I stepped back. I threw one sword to the ground, stepping on it. I raised the other two swords above me, glaring at the two remaining attackers, daring them to come close.

Behind me I heard an *oof* and a thudding noise. Sara had flipped the little attacker for a second time. I thrust the swords at the standing ninjas, and they froze, not coming any closer.

"Nice," I murmured.

"There will be others," she answered.

I looked down. Wait. *Sara* hadn't said that. The little attacker had.

But . . .

It was a woman's voice.

I used the tip of the Whisper to lift the mask off the little attacker. And when it came off, I gasped.

Mieko.

She stared up at us, her mouth cracked, her eyes crazy.

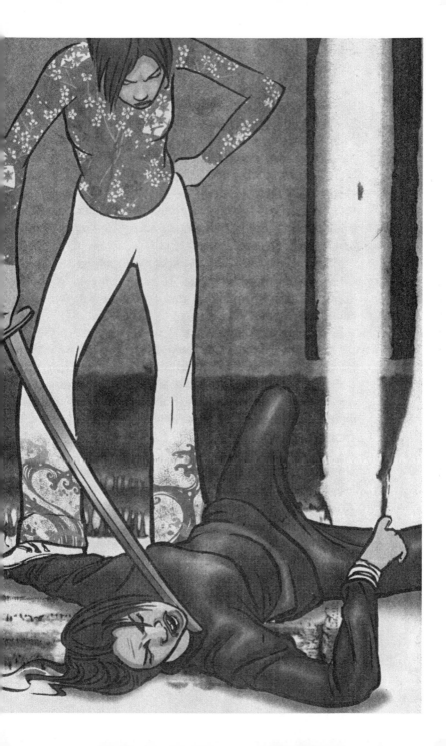

She saw Sara and her eyebrows curled together angrily.

"We finally meet," she said to Sara in Japanese.

I couldn't move. I turned my gaze very slowly over to the ninjas. But they weren't moving, either. The whole moment hung between Mieko and Sara, glaring at each other, years of hate welling up inside.

"I've always known about you," Mieko said. "So don't think you were doing anything too secretive. You can't even understand Japanese, I bet."

"Yes, I can," Sara answered back in Japanese.

Mieko narrowed her eyes. "You can, can you? Then you know the proper name for you. The name for you in my country. *Gaishou.*"

I clenched my fists. *Whore.*

"Kill her," I said. "She and her brother are killing my father. She and her brother killed Ohiko, too. You don't think I know, Mieko? You don't think I know what's going on?" Extreme anger welled up inside me. I *did* know my enemy. I'd known her all along. Mieko and Masato, trying to control the world.

"Kill her now," I said.

"That's right, go ahead, kill me," Mieko spat. She looked at me. "So, what's it like to have the love of your life betray you?" She smiled cruelly.

"Shut up!" I said.

"You should have seen him when he shook our hands," Mieko went on. "So proud. So dutiful to his father. He was a stupid boy not to follow through, but we got him in the end, didn't we!"

"You're not hurting me," I said. "Nothing you say can hurt me now."

Sara nodded for one of the swords. I handed her the Whisper. She held it inches from Mieko's throat.

"Kill her," I said again. "You are nothing," I told Mieko. "You and Masato. You are both absolutely nothing."

Sara stood there, the sword quivering. *If she doesn't kill her, I will,* I thought. But Sara continued to stand there, immobile.

"Your father never loved you," Mieko said to me. "And your brother never loved you. No one loved you!"

"No one loved you, either," I said in a calm voice.

For some reason, that got to her. Her expression changed from one of cold, heartless bitchiness to one of pathetic loneliness. It was incredible—it was as if Mieko's mask had been peeled away, and we were getting a glimpse of what a miserable person she was underneath.

She whimpered softly, her mouth mashing together.

"Come on, Sara," I whispered. "Come on, *Mom.*"

But Sara shook her head. "You're a sad little woman," she said. "You're right, Heaven. *No* one loves her."

Mieko's mouth moved frantically up and down. Sara turned the sword around. Now the blunt end faced Mieko's head. Sara raised it up and clubbed her with it, knocking her unconscious. Mieko fell awkwardly to the side.

Sara looked at me, shaken. We turned to the other attackers. No one moved. It was like they were in a suspended game of freeze tag.

"Come on," she said, grabbing my arm. "And take that."
She gestured to the Whisper.

I ran behind her, dragging the sword with me. "How did
you get the Whisper?" I asked.

"The car, the car. I'll tell you there."

"What about *her*?" I asked, looking at Mieko.

"We gotta split," she said, grabbing her keys and fling-
ing open the door.

"We can't just *leave* her," I said. But I knew. We couldn't
kill her, either. If we killed her, they'd find us. Fast. Masato
had sent his sister out to get slaughtered. He was still waiting for us. Somewhere.

We ran into the cool night air. Several attackers jumped
up, caught off guard. I raised the Whisper over my head;
Sara raised the sword that she'd pinched from Mieko. They
all took a step back. A few tried to rush us, but Sara nicked
them in the sides of their legs. They ran back, yelping in
pain. The others stayed put, immobile.

I threw the Whisper in the back of Sara's Audi and
noticed that Sam was lying in the backseat, curled up in a
ball, as if he'd known we would be going somewhere.

"Some attackers," Sara said. "Pretty lame, if you ask
me. You know, on the one-to-ten scale of attackers."

She pushed her key into the ignition and the Audi came
to life. "This thing goes pretty fast," she said. "So hold on."

"But where are we going?" I croaked. Were we just
going to leave Mieko in the house back there?

"I have it all planned out. I thought this might happen."

"You *did*?"

"We'll talk on the way. I know someone who can help us. There's this guy in Washington State who runs a dojo. It's actually on a little island off Seattle. Seriously, nothing happens there. Ever see *The Ring*?"

"Yeah . . . ," I said unsteadily.

"It's that island. It's completely remote. You have to get there by boat."

Oh God, another boat.

"We'll be totally safe," Sara said, noting my expression. "Don't worry."

"Okay," I said weakly.

At least, I thought, *I'm going with my mom. I'm not alone anymore.*

We backed out of the driveway to the yelling sounds of the attackers. "What will happen to your house?" I asked.

"It doesn't matter. Everything will be fine. Don't worry."

We *had* to run. I really would be running for the rest of my life.

"God," I said, putting my head in my hands. "What if they follow us?"

Suddenly Sara jerked on the brakes. I flew forward. The cat screeched.

"What the hell?" I said. *Someone's on the car,* I thought. *Hanging on to the back bumper with a gun in his hand. We're dead.*

I turned around slowly. No one. Empty road.

Then I whirled around to face the front. Someone was coming straight for us. Running at top speed. Right for the car. I thought I could see a gun.

"Go the other way!" I screamed. "It's Masato!"

But I couldn't really tell *who* it was. The only thing I could see was that this person who was coming was a guy. He looked angry.

"Back up, back up!" I said. It had to be Masato. A freakish thought occurred to me for a split second. *Was Sara against me, too?*

"It's not Masato," Sara said calmly. The person ran closer, out of the night shadows. He was big, tall, burly, with spiky hair.

"Oh my God," I whispered.

It was Teddy.

I think I screamed.

Teddy ran up to the car. "Hey," he said, out of breath. He looked at Sara, then looked at me. Then he smiled that crooked, lazy, Teddy Yukemura smile.

"What's up, Heaven?" He reached in and touched my hand.

"Teddy," I croaked. This was just a *little bit* too much for me to handle.

And then I noticed something else. On his wrist was the same thick leather band that Yoshitomo had been wearing. With the three dragons and everything. The same crazy detail.

"Where did you get that?" I said hysterically, pointing.

"Oh, a friend of mine," he said, winking. "Gave it to me right before he died."

My mouth hung open in disbelief. Wait. What? How did . . . ?

"Called me up, asking if I wanted to go in on a certain hit

on a certain person," Teddy said quickly. "Obviously he doesn't know me very well," he scoffed. "Idiot. You won't have to worry about him anymore."

Sara gunned the engine.

"I . . . ," I started, stunned.

"Girl, you look seriously freaked out," Teddy said, leaning over the window.

"Of *course* I'm seriously freaked out," I sputtered.

"And damn!" he interrupted. "You've been moving around so much! You're seriously *hard* to keep track of!"

"I . . . ," I mustered again. I glanced back at Sara's house. No one was coming after us. But would they soon?

"*You're* not hard to keep track of, Sara," he continued.

Sara?

I stared at both of them, and my mouth hung open. "You . . . *know* each other?" I said.

"Well, soon enough I'm going to be *majorly* hard to keep track of," Sara said. She looked at Teddy. He looked a little thin maybe and had a big cut running down his cheek, but otherwise he looked pretty good. He made me feel . . . I couldn't believe it . . . *turned on*. Nervous. Fluttery. He looked back at me and my heart flipped over. It felt almost . . . *thrilling*.

"Something went down?" Teddy asked.

"Yeah. The big one," Sara said. My head flicked back and forth between them as if I were watching a tennis match.

"So. You with us?" Sara asked Teddy.

He nodded.

"Well, then," she said, pointing to the backseat. "Get in."

Read an excerpt from

the latest book in the

exciting hit series

FEARLESS™

BOOK #32:
TERROR

A**ll** my life I've been like that rabbit from the Trix cereal commercials. We both spend our lives searching for one unattainable thing. We yearn and reach for it, only to watch it evaporate before our eyes like steam. All the Trix rabbit wants is a bowl of Trix, but my quest has been a little more complex. All I've ever wanted has been to experience fear.

I spent my first seventeen years plagued by *if* questions. If not for my fearlessness, would I have been so endlessly exploited? If I had been able to feel fear, would I have been better at letting down my emotional iron curtain? If I had been born with fear, would the three primary victims of my life—Heather, Sam, and Mary Moss—have been unharmed?

I thought I'd never know. I could buy a box of Trix whenever I wanted, but I would never know what fear felt like. When Loki injected me with that serum, what

I felt wasn't fear. It was a
paranoid-delusional, schizo-
phrenic, turbo-fueled version of
something far worse than fear.
What I craved was the real thing—
to be normal and fearful, like
everyone else. To sip from the
root beer float that is Jane
Normal's life. But I would never
know, because my genetic code was
tattooed inside me in some tiny,
inscrutable font. Even if someone
could have figured out what it
said, there wouldn't have been a
damn thing they could do about
it.

Until there was.

Until the Fates led me to the
Rodkes, that family in shining
armor. Until Dr. Rodke introduced
me to Dr. Ulrich, the grand sci-
entific mastermind who invented
the most advanced gene sequencer
on the planet. Thanks to him, I
have done it. I've reached my
personal holy grail. Less than
two days ago Dr. Ulrich injected
me with a sample of my own blood
that contained a corrected copy

of my genetic material as well as a carrier virus. The adenovirus acted as a superfast agent of the new DNA, starting a chain reaction of genetic regeneration in my sleeping body. And just like that—*wham*—my most salient trait was sucked right out of me. Soon after the anesthesia wore off, I, Gaia Moore, saw the first evidence of fear when I flinched at a high-pitched giggle.

What's it like for a fearless person to feel fear? It has its moments. There is a rekindled urgency in everything I do. Danger adds excitement. Watching *American Idol* last night, I kept cringing and half covering my eyes. And I kind of dug it. I've also noticed that the fear of losing Jake makes me want to find him and pull him close. That seems vaguely like the desire of a real girl.

So hooray for me, right? Way to go, Gaia. . . *right*? I've done the impossible, achieved the anti-me that I've always wanted to be. With the exception of a minor identity crisis, I should be in heavenly bliss now. I should be all smiles, born again, starting my life over from scratch. I should be Gaia 3.0, the new new me. I *should* be all these things.

But that would be entirely too convenient. And if there's one thing I've learned I can count on, it's inconvenience. Whenever things start to feel the slightest bit happy-go-lucky, I know I should duck for cover. Just as my relationship with Jake has become smooth sailing to an almost puke-worthy degree, just as I've taken this final step to becoming an anonymous every girl, of course something has to go and undermine it all. Just as I'm scooping out spoonfuls from that symbolic bowl of Trix drenched in delicious whole milk, I realize the milk is rancid. Every stroke of luck turns back to tragedy.

The facts are as follows: My fear told me to flee the scene of an attack last night, and the same attackers I didn't finish off attacked Ed and Kai immediately thereafter. Right now they're lying in St. Vincent's, and I'm. . . *not*. I'm walking fast through the city, knowing that the new me has failed her first test. Not too sweet. Being stripped of fearlessness is supposed to lower my profile. It's supposed to make me less hunted, to decrease the number of Gaia-related tragedies. . . .

But what if it doesn't? What if it just turns me into a total wuss who can't defend herself? What if I've made the wrong decision?

Protocol in romance wasn't exactly her strong point— reason number **the** two **paranoia** hundred and fourteen **front** why Gaia's relationships never worked out.

GAIA MOORE WAS TOO BUSY DOING

Sitting Ducks

the incognito speed walk to notice the weather. It was one of those gray, vaguely depressing Saturdays that New Yorkers knew all too well. There was the perfect amount of light out to render the Village mosaic of store-fronts, fire escapes, and sidewalk human activity in the crispest clarity. But she lurched forward on Hudson Street with such thrust that it strained her hips. Her head bowed like a bull's, she wove between pedestrians. Her eyes remained focused on the glittery, bubble-gum-peppered sidewalk that blurred beneath her feet. This was not the time to get distracted by the usual leather-faced homeless clump of a human or some smiling, lipsticked trannie. This was no time to experiment with fear. *Keep your eyes on the ground,* she told herself. Easy enough, for someone who could find St. Vincent's blindfolded.

As she walked, Gaia tried to conjure up an image of Ed's face. Unfortunately, her vision of him was blurred; it lacked specificity. Was he conscious? Would his eyes be open? And what about Kai? Gaia maneuvered around a slumped-over old woman. Just as she was about to merge back into the right pedestrian lane, she felt a flat thud on her upper left thigh.

"Ow," Gaia blurted.

She whirled around to check out the culprit. It was a briefcase, attached to the hand of some inconsiderate ass who hadn't bothered to apologize. *Sometimes I hate this place. There are so many people that no one notices you.*

Gaia started walking again and was struck by how slowly she was moving. *Am I procrastinating?* As much as she had to see Ed right now, she wasn't exactly looking forward to it. Was she scared? Was this fear—this gut-grinding, tight-gummed feeling of wanting to be somewhere else? Or was it dread? Maybe it was guilt. Guilt over her plan not to tell Ed and Kai that she'd run from the same attackers who'd later butchered them. A vision of Ed's back with the blood-encrusted *X* that had been slashed into it flashed through Gaia's mind, sending a shiver through her body.

Gaia suddenly stopped in her tracks. There was that feeling, one that Gaia had come to know all too well in her short time on earth. She felt an invisible force behind her, like two laser beams piercing the back of her brain. An unfathomable urge to sprint away rose up in her. *Is someone following me?* Probably not. It was just the fear talking. Every time she'd had a premonition or an eerie sensation in the past twenty-four hours, that had been her first thought. *It's just the fear talking.* It would have been nice to have a bottle of fear-relieving shampoo to rub on her scalp at times like this. Not to cure her of it entirely, but to alleviate the intensity.

She formulated a plan. At the count of three she would snap her head to the right, as if suddenly bedazzled by some eye-catching window display. *One. Two. Three.*

She stopped on a dime and turned. Out of the corner of her eye she saw a blur stream to the left and disappear. *Whisht.* Had it been a figment of her imagination? She quit feigning interest in the window and full-on stared down the street behind her. Nada. Just some hipster couple moseying along, pushing a baby carriage.

Gaia moved on, picking up the pace. *Please, not now.* Her spine felt tight. She felt like she needed a massage. Turning onto Eleventh Street, Gaia speeded up to a shuffle-jog. This was the homestretch. She took a wide, looping swath and looked down the block behind her, trying not to be blatant about it. *Boom.* There he was—a guy in a blue jacket. Was that her follower? Probably was, judging by the way he was pretending to look up at the buildings. *Don't panic, Gaia.*

The second she moved out of the stalker's vision, she broke into a sprint down Waverly. Ed would have to wait. The last thing she needed was for this guy to trace her to Ed's hospital room. Gaia's entire body tingled with adrenaline at the thought.

She crossed the street to the other sidewalk. The parked cars would help conceal her. She dodged slow-moving pedestrians, ran a quick sixty-yard dash, then ventured a look back. The follower was nowhere to be seen. But when she turned back around, she was staring into steel blue eyes.

"Oh my God!" Gaia yelled. For a split second she thought it was her father. She put a hand to her chest to soften the thumping of her lungs against her rib cage. A more probing look into his deep-set blue eyes showed that it wasn't her dad—it was Oliver.

"What are you doing, Oliver?" she said, still gasping. "You scared the crap out of me."

"Oh, I'm sorry." Oliver looked like he was forcing his face muscles into smiling position. "I was just thinking, What a pleasant surprise to run into my niece on the street."

Gaia felt pretty ridiculous. She really needed to take a chill pill. Then she noticed that Oliver's eyes matched his jacket. She felt hot bile churning in her stomach. *He's the follower.* "Right," she said. "What serendipity. Imagine the shock of running into someone you've been following for blocks."

"I don't know what you're talking about." Oliver raised his palms to proclaim innocence. "I live right near here. I was just walking around."

Gaia shot Oliver a suspicious glance. "I thought you said you moved to Broome Street."

"I did."

"That's down in SoHo," she said, knitting her brow. "It's not *that* nearby."

"Whatever you say." Oliver grabbed Gaia by the elbow. "I didn't come here to talk Manhattan geography—there's something much more important on my mind. But you seem a little agitated, Gaia. Are you okay?"

"I'm fine," Gaia lied. She knew she was probably overreacting, but this didn't feel quite right. Had Oliver been *following* following her or just hey-there's-my-niece-up-ahead following her?

"How about we step out into someplace less public so we can talk?" As Oliver guided Gaia by the elbow, it was he who seemed agitated.

Gaia pulled her arm away. "I can steer myself."

Oliver put up his hands. "Sorry. I'm just. . . a little tense, that's all. Not feeling so comfortable in crowds these days. You know how it is. I believe this is your street right here." Oliver pointed. "How about we duck down Bank?"

Gaia looked down Bank Street. It was a tree-canopied block, and the boardinghouse was still a few blocks away. As much as she trusted Oliver—these days, anyway—she wasn't in a state of mind to be stepping onto shady side streets with anyone. This next block had a total population of one—some guy throwing garbage bags onto a pile. Without consciously deciding to, Gaia started shaking her head. Why was he so insistent on privacy? Didn't the best intelligence operatives hide themselves in plain view? *Had* he been *following* her? And if so, why? Why didn't he just call her, like a normal human/uncle would?

"No. I'm sorry, but if you want to talk, we can talk right here," she said. There was an unintentional edge to her tone.

"Is something wrong, Gaia?" Oliver asked with sincere curiosity. "Why are you so fidgety?"

Gaia realized she was rocking back and forth on her heels and shaking her head like an autistic savant. "I'm fine. Nothing's wrong."

"Listen, Gaia, I feel that you're acting like you used to act around Loki. But I'm not here to hurt you." The softness of his voice caught Gaia's attention. Loki wasn't capable of such a soft voice. "Quite the opposite. I'm trying to make up for lost time and finally be the uncle you need me to be. I'm here to protect you, especially with your father away."

"That's considerate of you," Gaia said. "But I told you, I can protect myself."

"You're wrong. You have no idea." Oliver's voice had risen a few octaves. It was as if some inner switch had been flipped. He sounded like a beleaguered teenager whining about his curfew. "If you keep making these visits to St. Vincent's, you'll *definitely* need my protection. Is that where you're going right now?"

"Whoa." *Does he know about the procedure?* She took a moment to put one finger in the air, trying to process what Oliver had said. Her paranoia seemed suddenly justified. "Wait a second. You really *have* been following me."

"No." Oliver's eyes started darting in a way that implied he was telling a half-truth. "Not me personally, anyway. . ."

"Great," Gaia said. "Which means you have operatives. I thought you were going to lay low, Oliver. Avoid using your old resources. The Agency told you to."

"Look, Gaia, I don't have to listen to the Agency anymore. That's the whole point. I'll do whatever it takes to keep you safe, even if it's a risk for me. That's a covenant I've made with myself. And I plan to stick to it."

Gaia looked into his eyes. Having operatives follow her felt distinctly like a Loki move. But the strength of Oliver's conviction, as exhibited by his steely blue-eyed gaze, was persuasive. If his intentions were bad, then he was a hell of an actor. And having witnessed firsthand how formidable a foe Oliver could be, it was nice to have him on her team now. Besides, who knew? Maybe he was right. She had just been attacked. Maybe she should lighten up on the paranoia front. Maybe she did need him.

"Okay," Gaia said. "So what do you think I should do?"

"I think you should leave New York," he said without the slightest hesitation.

"What?" Gaia asked, immediately dismayed. "When?"

"Tonight. With me."

Gaia didn't even have to think about that one. Almost every time she left the city with her uncle, she seemed to end up strapped to a table in a dingy warehouse somewhere. Not that she still distrusted him like that. But this was the last thing she needed right now, just as she was about to embark on a life of normalcy. And the thought of leaving Jake at this point was outright repugnant. "I can't do that," she said flatly.

"*Gaia*," Oliver said, his tone suddenly impatient. "I can't keep watch over you every second of every hour, and New York right now is a hotbed of enemy agents."

"How do you know?" Gaia said. "Who's the enemy? And why are you so sure they want me?"

"I haven't fully figured that out, but I have some ideas. All I know for sure is that you're not safe in Manhattan."

But that's where I live. Gaia realized this conversation was a dead end. She couldn't leave New York, period, because it was the only place in the world where someone as abnormal as she could try her hand at being normal. If someone was after her, she would just have to be more careful. For now, though, this wasn't the most important issue in her life.

To suddenly split town because her wild-eyed uncle was raving about some imagined apocalypse was exactly what she *didn't* need. "Listen, Oliver." She put her hand on his shoulder to loosen him up. "I appreciate you looking out for me and all, but I have something else to attend to right now. A friend needs me. And as for leaving Manhattan with you, all I can say is that it's not happening. But thanks. . ."

Gaia flashed Oliver her best sympathetic smile and shouldered past him.

OLIVER GRABBED GAIA'S SHOULDER FROM

behind and jerked her to a standstill. He didn't use enough force to hurt her, just enough to let her know he meant business. She couldn't just walk away from him. He was trying to help.

"Please don't grab me," Gaia said, and Oliver could hear that she meant it.

"I'm sorry. I was just trying to get your attention."

Sometimes force was necessary to get a point across. Oliver knew this as well as anyone. As Loki, he had used force to manipulate all kinds of situations, usually to further some evil scheme. But rarely had he felt the need to use force to protect someone from harm. It was a confusing dilemma, too, because verbal logic didn't seem to work in persuading Gaia of the danger she was in. He also knew for a fact that she didn't respond well to force. But *something* had to be done.

"I think you're in serious danger. I've been tracking those two phony agents who came asking about you, and I don't like the looks of it. I'm pretty certain you'll be their next target. We need to discuss this."

Gaia's arms were wrapped around her chest but more in a comforting than a defiant way. "I'm supposed to be somewhere. . . right now, actually." She looked at her watch. "I'm already late."

"Hey. Don't blow me off, Gaia." Oliver could feel his patience slipping. He lowered his tone. "Just because you're brave doesn't make you immortal."

The look on Gaia's face was something he'd never seen before. That last line seemed to have hit her hard. If he hadn't known her better, he would've called it *pure terror.* Which made no sense, but at least he was getting through to her. Then again, her facial expression was now morphing like a fast-moving storm cloud toward something like angry resentment.

"I'm not kidding, Gaia," he said. "These people are playing for keeps. My research shows that big money and lots of people are behind this movement. And judging from the attacks so far, they're not out to send

messages. They're totally prepared to liquidate whoever gets in their way."

Gaia was sucking on the inside of her cheek. Oliver
had seen her do this. It meant that he had her attention. "So," she said. "What do you want me to do? You
keep talking about *they,* but who are *they?* I guess I can
take your word that someone's out there, but still,
your accusations are so vague that I wouldn't even
know who to watch out for."

"Fair enough." Oliver put up his hands in a concil-
iatory gesture. She seemed willing to cooperate now.
He had pierced the outer layer of her armor. "Maybe if
you answered a question or two, it would help lead me
toward some more specific answers. . . ."

"So shoot," Gaia said.

"Who have you been visiting at the hospital?"
Oliver asked.

"I can't say."

"You should be wary of letting doctors get too
familiar with your body," he said. "If they find out how
unique you are, you'll spend the rest of your life as a
science project."

"You don't think I'm aware of that?" Gaia asked
loudly. "If that's all you came to say, you can just save
your breath."

Oliver felt the urge to pound something. That was
another thing that hadn't changed over the years—
Gaia's ability to irritate him to the

boiling point with that petulant tone of hers. *Calm yourself,* Oliver thought. *If you get pissed, you'll lose her.* She was getting defensive, though, which meant he'd hit a nerve. He exhaled. "Please, at the very least, do your uncle the favor of lowering your voice in public. I don't think it *that* odd to want a little privacy for our conversation. Do you? I assure you that it's not an uncomplicated matter. So let's just sit on a stoop here or maybe walk to a quiet coffee shop if you want where we can discuss things."

"Sorry," Gaia said. "But it's not a good time."

"Are you going to St. Vincent's?" Oliver asked.

"No...," she said. "Maybe. Why does that matter?"

"Maybe it doesn't," Oliver said. "I don't know. I just want a few minutes of your time."

"Which I've already granted," Gaia snapped, looking at her watch again. "As I said before, I'm late. And this person is not in the best of health."

Oliver felt himself boiling over. He grabbed Gaia by both shoulders. He stared into her eyes, hoping to mesmerize her. "Whoever it is can wait a few more minutes. It's not Jake, is it?"

"Don't worry about it," Gaia said. Oliver sensed she was slipping away. "Look, you can send me an e-mail as soon as you know more details about this new enemy on the streets. That's the best way to get ahold of me. E-mail."

Gaia started to walk away. *She needs to hear this,*

Oliver thought. His instincts told him to grab her, but reason took hold. He hustled in front of her and started walking alongside her. "You have two options. You can leave the city now or go into the thick of battle with an unknown, yet populous army. Take your pick."

"Leave. Me. Alone."

"I can't," Oliver said. "I don't know what it is, but I sense that you're particularly vulnerable right now. You have to watch your back."

"I will."

Oliver was suddenly consumed by urgent rage. His eyes widened, and he stepped toward Gaia. It took some mental control to keep from literally shaking sense into her. "Ignoring this warning could be suicide, Gaia. Don't do it."

"Message received. Danger duly noted. But I really have to go, Oliver. And if you don't stop harassing me, I'm going to run."

"Don't do that." Oliver felt the breath forcing its way out of his nostrils. His patience was almost used up. He was on the verge of getting extremely pissed, and once he got to that point, there was no telling what he'd do. Apparently sensing this fact, Gaia took off in a sprint. Oliver's instincts took over and he ran after her. But just as he was beginning to bridge the gap, he realized how ridiculous he was being. *What am I going to do, tackle her?*

Oliver shuffled to a stop. He looked around him to make sure there were no significant witnesses. No cops. Watching her sprint away, he considered following her. But he couldn't. A full-speed chase through the Village would have been more than just a little suspicious. *Damn it!* Oliver kicked a metal trash can. A stuffed bag flew out and the can rolled to the bottom of the curb, then back and forth in a semicircle. When had Gaia turned into such a jittery ball of nerves? Why was she being so defensive? Stupid girl. It was just a matter of time before those fake agents got to her, and then she'd be wishing she'd skipped town with her uncle. When they turned her into their personal lab rat, she'd be wishing she hadn't been such a stupid, insolent little brat.